camp CONFIDENTIAL

Second Summer

Second Time's the Charm

Visit us at www.abdopublishing.com

Reinforced library bound edition published in 2009 by Spotlight, a division of ABDO Group, 8000 West 78th Street, Edina, Minnesota 55439. This library bound edition is published by arrangement with Grosset & Dunlap, a member of Penguin Group (USA) Inc.

Front cover image © Photodisc Photography/Getty Images/Veer Incorporated. Text copyright © 2006 by Grosset & Dunlap. All rights reserved. Published by Grosset & Dunlap, a division of Penguin Young Readers Group, 345 Hudson Street, New York, NY 10014. GROSSET & DUNLAP is a trademark of Penguin Group (USA) Inc.

Library of Congress Cataloging-in-Publication Data
This title was previously cataloged with the following information:
Morgan, Melissa J.
  Second time's the charm / by Melissa J. Morgan.
  p. cm. -- (Camp Confidential ; 7)
  Summary: Having returned for her second year at Camp Lakeview, Natalie finds herself feeling jealous of a new camper from California who seems to be even more sophisticated and glamorous than Natalie, herself.
  [1. Jealousy--Fiction. 2. Camps--Fiction. 3. Friendship--Fiction. 4. Pennsylvania--Fiction.] I. Title. II. Series.
PZ7.M82545 Sec 2006
[Fic]--dc22   2005033180

ISBN: 0-448-44265-5 (paperback)
ISBN: 978-1-59961-507-3 (reinforced library bound edition)

All Spotlight books have reinforced library binding and are manufactured in the United States of America.

camp
CONFIDENTIAL

Second Summer

Second Time's the Charm

by Melissa J. Morgan

Grosset & Dunlap

chapter

Dear Hannah,

I guess sometimes the truth really
is stranger than fiction, huh? I mean, if
this time last year you had told me that
I would be RETURNING to Camp Lake-
puke—voluntarily, no less—I would have
laughed in your face. And then run away
crying.

And yet. Here I am, crowded onto
a smelly, oversized charter bus and
surrounded by kids singing "Ninety-Nine
Bottles of Beer on the Wall" at the top of
their lungs. And even though they are only

at eighty-seven bottles, and even though some of these kids couldn't make the first cut of <u>American Idol</u>, I don't have the vaguest impulse to scream. In fact, I'm feeling pretty zen. I even chimed in for a bar or two, somewhere back around ninety-one bottles or so.

Pretty amazing, huh?

Not only am I not hating the thought of coming back to camp, I'm even excited about it! Mom shipped me a survival kit of soy chips and PowerBars well in advance this time around. No more tuna surprises for me! And I am all stocked up on magazines. Alyssa's here sitting next to me—she says "hi"—and Grace is somewhere up front, leading a small faction of non-singers in a rousing game of bus charades. It's hilarious. And I can't wait to see the rest of the girls:

Jenna, Valerie, Sarah, Alex, and the other 3C-ers.

And, um, a particular boy.

Yes, Simon. He's been awesome about writing and calling, as you know, but we've only seen each other once in person since the reunion. I'm going into serious withdrawal. I really, really hope he's as excited to see me as I am to see him. But only time will tell, right? Right. I wish you were here to give me one of your patented pep talks.

In case you haven't noticed, I'm a little nervous.

Who am I kidding? Of course you've noticed—Simon's all we ever talk about. Bless you, you're a good friend . . .

Anyway, the natives are getting restless, which must mean that we're almost there. That, and Alyssa just told me that we're *almost there. See how smart I am?*

I'd better sign off. Try not to miss me too much while you're strolling along the Champs-Elysées, eating chocolate croissants and shopping till you drop. Feel free to send me some French chocolate whenever the spirit moves you.

> *Write soon,*
> *Nat*

Natalie Goode capped her purple felt-tipped pen, folded her letter to her best friend, Hannah, into quarters, and tucked it into the front pouch of her backpack. She sighed contentedly. Hannah was spending the summer in France with her mother, a super-glamorous foreign ambassador. Hannah's parents traveled a ton for work, and so over the summers they preferred to travel *with* their daughter, preferably to various exotic locales.

Not Natalie's parents, though. Natalie's mother was an art buyer, and summers were her time to scout new talent. And Natalie's father . . . well, he had a pretty offbeat career.

Natalie's father was Tad Maxwell, a hugely famous movie star who mostly appeared in big-time action movies. He lived in L.A. full-time but was on the road a lot, shooting on location and doing press junkets for his various movies and stuff. Natalie missed him of course, but her parents had gotten divorced when she was pretty young, and so by now she was used to the situation. Her dad loved her; she knew that beyond a shadow of a doubt, and she never took for granted the time they had together.

In fact, for Natalie, the biggest thing about having a famous father was worrying what other kids would think of her. At her school, lots of kids had parents who were ultra-wealthy or had super-high-powered jobs and stuff. So they didn't think anything of the fact that Natalie's father was a movie star. But she never knew how other people—and, in particular, new people—would react. That was one of the reasons Natalie had been so nervous last summer when her mother had shipped her off to Camp Lakeview—or "Lake-puke," as Nat had affectionately come to call it (the other reason had to do with a deathly aversion to "the Great Outdoors" that Nat had since gotten over—kind of.).

When Natalie thought about how totally unenthusiastic she had been about camp last summer, she had to laugh. After all, she'd made some amazing friends at Lakeview, and learned a lot about herself in the process. Okay, sure, people were *slightly* weirded out when they found out the truth about her father, but her friends—her *real* friends—were mostly just disappointed that she hadn't felt that she could con-fide in them. And, besides, that was all over now, anyway. Her secret was out in the open. *Way* out in the open. Natalie wondered if her friend Alex, a Lakeview legacy and soccer champ, had brought her Tad Maxwell poster back to camp this summer. *Or maybe she even got a new one,* Nat thought. Alex could be a little bit bossy sometimes, so she and Nat had had their share of friction now and then, but she was a dedicated camper and a supremely loyal friend. Natalie was psyched to be bunking with her again this summer.

"I can't wait to see Jenna," Alyssa said, rousing Natalie from her internal monologue. "She told me she bought a book of practical jokes that she's dying to try out."

"Jenna should know better than that," Natalie quipped. Their fellow 3C-er was a noted prankster whose jokes had not gone without consequence the summer before. Of course, her good humor was so infectious that it was difficult to stay upset with her for too long.

"Anyway, she told me that she would meet us at the great field, where the buses let out," Alyssa continued. She pointed out the streaky, tinted window. "Can you see her?" she asked, cupping her eyes against the glass and squinting outward. Their bus was, at present, rumbling to a halt along the field. Somehow, while Natalie had been lost in her daydream, they had arrived at camp!

"Yeah, she's . . ." Natalie's voice trailed off as she broke out laughing. "She's the one tap-dancing down the path. Minus the tap shoes." She giggled again as their friend made her way into the melee of the great field, kicking up great clouds of dust as she moved forward.

Their bus screeched to a halt, coughing exhaust fumes and sputtering as the engine died. The campers cried out, jumping out of their seats and moving eagerly toward the door. "One at a time," their bus counselor, Pete, begged in vain. Pete was a member of the kitchen staff who was so good-natured that it was hard to hold his terrible cooking against him.

"I call bottom bunk," Natalie shouted, playfully shoving past Alyssa and bounding down the steps of the bus.

"Hey, no fair calling the bunk before it's in sight," Alyssa protested, hot on Natalie's heels.

"Jenna!" Natalie shrieked, flinging her arms around her friend as though they hadn't seen each other in ages. *Which, come to think of it, we haven't,* Natalie realized. The last time their entire bunk had been together had been at the camp reunion—back in February! "Did you see our bunk yet? Is it nicer than last year's bunk? Is there mold in the showers? Are the screen windows torn?" The perma-smile faded from Jenna's face, prompting Natalie's suspicion. "Oh, no. *Is* there mold in the showers?"

Jenna shook her head slowly. She wasn't tap-dancing anymore. Natalie had a feeling that whatever Jenna had to tell her, it was pretty serious. "Oh, no," Natalie teased, trying to lighten the mood. "Are there *spiders* in the showers?"

Jenna smiled, but it was a weak smile at best. *This has got to be bad news,* Natalie thought, a cold fist of dread settling into her stomach like a lead weight.

Alyssa, always no-nonsense, adjusted her tote bag over her shoulder and stepped forward, hands on her hips like she meant business. "Come on, Jenna. Worse than spiders? Spill."

"It's our bunk, 4A," Jenna said, looking much more somber than Natalie could ever recall seeing her.

"What, did we get, like, an awful counselor or something?" Natalie asked, growing increasingly worried. An awful counselor could really be a bad omen, as far as enjoyment of the summer was concerned.

"Well, no. At least, as far as I know," Jenna said nervously. Natalie raised an eyebrow quizzically. "It's just—" Jenna finally blurted. "Our bunk!" she sputtered. "We're not all together this summer."

"You mean—" Alyssa cut in anxiously.

"Exactly," Jenna said, shaking her head. "We've been split up!"

TWO

Natalie took one look at Jenna's woeful expression and burst out laughing. "Sure, yeah, whatever," she giggled. "Good one, Jenna." She slapped her friend lightly on the shoulder. "Weren't you going to try to stay out of trouble this year?" she chided. "We haven't even gotten to the bunk yet and you're already making with the funny? Which, by the way, is *so* not that funny," she added, mock-stern.

When Jenna didn't respond—and certainly not with anything resembling Natalie's laugher—the sense of foreboding returned to Natalie's insides and she revisited her original idea that perhaps the noted prankster was, for once in her life, being serious. Natalie raised an eyebrow, still half skeptical. "No kidding?"

Jenna shook her head ruefully. "I wish. But not."

"How does that happen?" Alyssa asked. "I thought we all requested each other."

Jenna shrugged unhappily. "It's not, like, a

surefire system. I mean, they do the best that they can." She sighed.

"I guess we just have to deal," Alyssa said, pragmatic as always. "Are Nat and I in the same bunk?"

Jenna nodded, clearly happy to finally be delivering some good news. "Yeah, in 4A, with me. We're with Karen and Jessie, too. And some new girls."

"That sounds cool," Natalie said. "Wait—" she paused, realizing. "Did Chelsea come back?"

"Yup," Jenna confirmed. "She's with us, too."

Natalie groaned. Chelsea was a difficult camper at best. Spoiled and petty, Chelsea loved to give her bunkmates the hardest time possible. They tried to reach out to her, but their efforts almost always backfired. Meanwhile, over the winter, Chelsea's father had been very sick. The girls of 3C had banded together during the weekend of the Lakeview reunion to show Chelsea how much they cared about her, but even that hadn't gone off without a hitch. They'd gotten through to the prickly girl, but it wasn't any sort of big, fuzzy lovefest. And there was no telling how Chelsea was going to behave now that they were back at camp.

"Well, supposedly her dad's doing much better," Jenna said. "Which is awesome. And could go a long way toward improving her mood."

"That'd be nice," Alyssa said absently. "Let's get our stuff and go over and find out the bunk assignments. Jenna can fill us in on the way. Look, Nat, there's your duffel." She pointed off toward the side of the bus, where, indeed, Natalie's enormous pink oversized bag was being tossed out from the bus's underneath storage compartment. "Um, did you pack, like, your entire bedroom? I mean, most of our stuff was supposed to be shipped here separately a week ago. And that looks like more than 'most' to me." She smiled to show that she was semi-teasing, but Natalie wouldn't have been offended, anyway.

"Maybe half my bedroom," Natalie admitted. "I mean, you never know what you're going to need."

"Or who you're going to see," Jenna teased. "Like, maybe someone whose name rhymes with *lymon.*"

"Ha-ha," Natalie said, ignoring her friend but still not exactly disagreeing with her, either. She was dying to see Simon, and there was no attempting to hide that from her friends. "Anyway, I get the hint, Alyssa. Let's grab our bags and head over to the bunk. I mean, we should make the best of this situation. It's not the end of the world for us all to be separated. It'll be fun to meet new people this summer."

"That's the spirit," Alyssa said, clapping Natalie on the back. "And you know what else will be fun?"

"What?" Natalie asked.

"Watching you carry that bag all by yourself," Alyssa cracked.

At that, Natalie could do little more than giggle. And grit her teeth as she prepared to hoist The Bag That Ate New York all the way from the bus to the bunk area.

"And then Alex, Brynn, Valerie, Sarah, Grace,

and Candace are in 4C," Jenna explained as the girls made their way up the front steps of their home for the summer. "With, um, you know that girl Gaby from bunk 3A last year?" She wrinkled her nose. Gaby was known for being sort of a bully, and she and Grace had had kind of a falling-out the summer before.

"I'm sure Grace is super-thrilled," Natalie said, slightly sarcastically.

"Well, Grace always gets it together to be cheery and make the best of a situation," Alyssa said.

"That's the understatement of the year," Natalie replied, thinking of Grace's endless good humor and wacky, dramatic flair. "Yeah, if anyone will be fine dealing with Gaby, it'll be Grace. Anyway"—she squared her shoulders, taking in the slightly saggy front porch of the bunk—"this cabin's not half as run-down as 3C was."

"I will reserve judgment until I see the showers," Alyssa quipped.

"Good call," Natalie agreed. "Ugh. I'm dying. Can we *please* go inside so that I can put this bag down once and for all?"

Alyssa nodded. "But let that be a lesson to you," she said, waving grandiosely toward her own smaller, wheeled, and overall much-more-practical duffel.

Natalie shook her head and followed her friends into Bunk 4A.

The upshot to being a fourth-division camper was easily apparent. For starters, as Natalie had noticed, the building itself was in moderately better condition. Nothing to write home about, but still. There weren't any visible holes in the window screens or anything like that, which was a step up, to be sure. Second of all, each of the girls got double the cubby space that she'd had last summer. This was great news, particularly in light of the size of Natalie's duffel bag. Nat would have liked it if, like the fifth-division campers, they could have been allotted more single beds, but since she knew Alyssa would take the top bunk, anyway, it really wasn't an issue. The top bunk was fun to hang out on, but Natalie had a deathly—if irrational—fear of falling out of bed in the middle of the night. She didn't know what would happen if one were to fall out of the top bunk, but she also wasn't in any rush to find out anytime soon.

"Wanna go check out the bathrooms?" Alyssa asked, prodding Natalie in the side and breaking her reverie.

Natalie shook her head no. "It's bound to be bad news, and I'd rather prolong the inevitable. Ignorance is bliss."

"Smart move. I learned the hard way about daddy longlegs with their own zip code."

Natalie looked up to see a stunning blonde standing before her, holding up a lip gloss palate that Natalie knew for a fact had just been released from Sephora online the day before. "*Where* did you get that?" she asked, willing herself not to drool. "Barneys isn't taking advance orders for another week." This girl obviously had connections. Highly not fair.

"Fred Segal," the girl said, shrugging somewhat apologetically. "I'm from Los Angeles." She pointed at her tank top, which was baby blue and indeed read "LA SURF SHOP" right across the chest in white stenciling.

"Oh," Natalie said, mildly disappointed, both about the lip gloss and about her sure-to-be-new-friend's origins. "I thought you totally had to be another New Yorker. So the lip gloss hit the West Coast before the East?" *Big-time* not fair.

"Not really," the girl explained, smiling. "I mean, you were right when you said it wasn't out yet. My mom is a beauty editor for an online magazine out in California. She gets to test everything out in advance. I mean, everything. So I've got lots and lots of junk lying around. You're welcome to borrow it," she said, as though it were no big deal. *Which, to her, it probably isn't,* Natalie thought incredulously. To have access to any beauty product you wanted—even in advance of the rest of the world? To Natalie, that would be heaven. She only hoped this girl—whose name was still a mystery—had some idea of how lucky she was.

"You're from California and you came all the way out *here* for camp?"

Natalie would have recognized that saccharine-sweet tone anywhere. "Hi, Chelsea," she said, thinking, *Way to make a new camper feel right at home.* Though, come to think of it, a crash course in Chelsea 101 was probably a good idea.

If the new girl was fazed by Chelsea's rudeness, she didn't show it. "Well, yeah. I mean, my mom and dad are out in L.A.—he's an entertainment lawyer—but my mom grew up in Philly and used to come to Lakeview, like, forever, when she was growing up. So once they decided I was old enough for sleepaway camp, there was no question that I was coming here. I'm Tori, by the way," she said, grinning and exposing the gleaming white teeth of a genuine California beach bunny.

"You're plenty old enough for sleepaway camp," Chelsea grumbled, wandering off toward her bed to unpack. Clearly she was bored with the conversation.

Natalie rolled her eyes in Chelsea's direction, hoping to make the point that the sourpuss was not to be taken seriously. "I'm Natalie," she said, extending a well-manicured hand for a shake. "And I'm *really* excited to use your lip gloss."

Tori laughed. "Seriously, anytime," she said. "But here's my question . . ."

"Shoot," Natalie said, thinking back to when she'd first arrived at Lakeview, totally overwhelmed. She was 150 percent ready to help Tori get the lay of the land—and she knew Alyssa would be, too.

Tori swept her gaze across the dusty floor and rusty bedsprings. Her aqua eyes sparkled in good-natured dismay. "Is this really where we . . . *sleep?*"

Natalie cracked up. After all, she could totally relate. Totally. "It is," she confirmed. She giggled again. "But don't worry. You get used to it."

▲ ▲ ▲

Bunk 4A's counselor for the summer was Andie, a short, bubbly girl with auburn hair, friendly brown eyes, and a smattering of freckles across her nose. Their CIT, or counselor-in-training, Mia, was tall and athletic, with straight, sun-streaked blond hair, deep emerald eyes, and very tanned skin. She had been a lifeguard at her pool for a few weeks before the summer started, she explained, as if she needed an excuse for looking like a refugee from *The OC*. Andie and Mia were both new to Lakeview, which Jenna assured the other girls was good news since they'd be, in her own words, "more pushover-y." Nat wasn't so sure, but they both seemed very nice, anyway.

As Jenna had explained, Jessie and Karen were both in 4A, as well as Perry, Anna, Lauren, and, of course, Tori. Perry, Anna, Lauren, and Tori were all new.

After everyone had arrived and mostly unpacked (Nat noted with relief that Karen had apparently left the bulk of her considerable stuffed animal collection at home this summer), Andie held a quick bunk meeting, where they introduced themselves more formally. Everyone knew that the real "getting to know you" would take place at the division-wide cookout that night, with icebreakers and the real treat: s'mores. Nat grinned to herself just thinking about s'mores. You could get them at certain funky coffee shops in New York City, but she wouldn't want to. They were such a total camp thing.

"Girls," Andie shouted, clapping her hands together in a burst of enthusiasm, "lunchtime!"

Alyssa groaned. "What are the odds that the food improved since last summer?"

"Slim to none," Nat replied quickly. "I mean, really." She turned to Tori. "Stick with us," she warned the new girl. "You'll need the moral support."

Tori's eyes widened. "That bad?"

Natalie nodded. "Trust us."

"Got it," Tori said. She ran her fingers through her hair quickly. "Am I a mess? Do I need to, I don't know, do something?"

Alyssa shook her head. "You're totally presentable. Red-carpet ready."

"Oh, no," Jenna whined, chiming in. "Are you another one of those? All into makeup, and hair, and clothes, and . . . *boys*?" She asked this last bit of her question as though it were the worst possible accusation. Jenna was a major tomboy and could not for her life understand her friends' interest in the opposite sex. She tolerated their crushes . . . but just barely.

Tori shrugged. "Guilty as charged."

"Of course. Just what we needed: a Natalie 2.0." It was Chelsea, of course, always needing to insert her own two cents.

"Whatever, Chelsea," Natalie said. She obviously couldn't care less what Chelsea thought of her.

But . . .

On the one hand, it was awesome to have someone around who was from a big city, and who understood the finer subtleties of beauty products— she bet that Tori had an awesome stash of teen mags hidden away somewhere, too—but on the other hand, being the chic, sophisticated urbanite was sort of Natalie's. . . *thing*. She wasn't totally sure that she was ready to share it.

Whatever. As quickly as the thought had popped into her head, she willed it gone. Tori seemed cool, and Natalie was psyched to get to know her. Natalie totally wasn't the jealous type. That would be ridiculous.

Right?

▲ ▲ ▲

"Grace!" Natalie let out an enthusiastic shriek and darted down the dirt path that wound from the bunks to the mess hall. Pandemonium ensued, campers hollering, hugging, and clapping one another on the back, commenting on haircuts, wardrobes, highlights from the school year past. 3C had kept a blog online over the course of the year where they could post shout-outs and updates to one another, but there was nothing like some good old-fashioned face time. The Internet, Natalie mused, would never really substitute for actual human interaction. Though she and her friends were lucky to have it when they couldn't see one another in person.

"Hey!" Grace called out, jogging over from where her own bunk was congregated. "Did you say hi to everyone else?"

Natalie shook her head. "Just got down here. Bummer that we're split up," she said.

"Seriously." Grace put the back of her hand to her forehead like a heroine from an old movie. "No, seriously," she said, straightening up. "It's totally annoying."

Natalie smiled sympathetically, then lowered her voice to a whisper: "How is it with Gaby?"

"Oh, whatever. I think it's going to be the way

it always was with Chelsea. You know—grin and make the best of it."

Natalie giggled. "Shh," she warned. "Don't want her to hear you. We have to get off on the right foot. New summer, fresh start, etc. . . ."

"Good point," Grace said, saluting and making one of her "Grace-faces." She turned toward her bunkmates and beckoned them to her. Soon Natalie, Alyssa, and Jenna were reunited with their old friends.

"So who's new in 4C?" Jenna asked.

"Tiernan and Abby," Alex said authoritatively. Alex loved nothing more than a chance to be authoritative. *Most of the time it's cute,* Natalie thought. *Most of the time.* "And Priya from last year," Alex continued.

Priya had been at Lakeview the previous summer, but she'd been in bunk 3B, and so neither Nat nor any of her friends had gotten to know her very well. Natalie remembered being very impressed by Priya's skin, which was always clear and rosy. Too bad that she was such a tomboy that she didn't fully appreciate her good fortune. Priya was notable for being BFF with a *boy.* His name was Jordan and they did everything together, though they swore they were *just friends.*

"What about your counselors?" Jenna asked.

"Oh, we've got Becky, and then Sophie is our CIT," Alex said. Becky was a longtime counselor who was a favorite among the campers, and Sophie had been a camper herself in the oldest division the summer before. "They're really cool."

"Awesome," Natalie said. "We've got Andie and Mia. They're both new."

"You know what that means," Jenna cackled, rubbing her hands together with glee.

"You promised you would behave," Natalie reminded her friend. "No more repeats of horrible pranks gone awry, like last year."

"Spoil my fun, why don't you," Jenna said, pouting. "Fine." She folded her arms across her chest.

"We've got some cool new girls in our bunk, too," Natalie said. "You have to meet Tori. She's from L.A.—very Hollywood."

"Really? How much Hollywood can one camp have?" Brynn teased, tossing her head and fluffing her bright red hair in the breeze. Like Grace, Brynn loved drama and could always be counted on to be very over-the-top. "Wait, I take that back. Maybe it's my chance to be discovered. The more Hollywood, the better! Bring her on!"

Natalie laughed. "Definitely." She craned her neck, trying to pick Tori out of the crush of campers. "I have no idea where she went. Oh—there!" she said, spotting her friend. "Tori—come up and meet the 4C-ers!"

Tori looked up from where she stood and, catching Natalie's eye, smiled and ran toward the girls. "Hey," she said, grinning warmly at the others. "I'm Tori."

Natalie introduced her friends quickly. "Don't worry, there won't be, like, a quiz or anything later," she joked.

"I'm good with names," Tori assured her. "I have a great memory. It's a little weird."

"So where'd you disappear to?" Nat asked. "I turned around and—poof—you were gone!"

"Oh, well, I had a little situation," Tori said, lowering her voice.

"Uh-oh, what happened?" Jenna asked, looking worried.

Tori chuckled. "Nothing like that," she said. "It was, like, a big-time Hottie Alert. I felt it was my duty to scope out the situation."

"How big of you," Alyssa said drily.

Natalie shoved her friend lightly. "I, for one, appreciate the gravity of the Hottie Alert," she said, very serious. The twinkle in her eye gave her away, however. "Show me!" she squealed, grabbing on to Tori's arm.

"Oh, yeah, you'll need a full visual," Tori said. "I don't think mere words could do him justice." She scanned the crowd again. "He was just standing over by the pagoda, sort of by himself. If he's still there, it's the perfect opportunity to go over and say hi. He was, like, thin, with these awesome blue eyes. Light brown hair. You know . . . your basic hottie."

A suspicious feeling settled into the pit of Natalie's stomach. She knew a certain blue-eyed someone who loved to hang out by the pagoda, often by himself. But then, what were the odds . . . *there must a ton of blue-eyed boys here at Lakeview.*

"That's him! Couldn't you just *die*?" Tori shrieked, waking Nat from her little internal monologue.

Natalie whipped her head around. All at once, her worst instincts were confirmed. Never again would she brush aside that twinge of suspicion in her gut. She hated to believe it, but the truth was right there, in front of her face. She was looking directly at Tori's new crush.

She was looking directly at *Simon*!

"It's, like, a travesty, right?" Tori said, squeezing Natalie's arm so hard, Nat thought she'd lose circulation. "Such adorableness should not be standing there all by himself."

Perfect, Natalie thought. *This girl is checking out my maybe-boyfriend, and meanwhile I'm the one losing blood supply to my outer limbs.*

She gently extricated herself from Tori's death-grip of love, wondering what the best, most graceful way would be to handle the situation. How to break the news to Tori that, in fact, the hottie she was scoping out was spoken for? Sort of. Maybe.

"Oh, that's *perfect.*"

Somehow, Chelsea had crept up behind the girls and witnessed this completely awkward moment. She was grinning at Nat and Tori like the cat that had eaten the canary. "I guess there just aren't enough boys to go around. What a shame," she said, widening her eyes innocently before slinking off.

"What is she talking ab—oh, no," Tori said, realization dawning. She clapped one hand over her mouth. "Tell me I'm checking out your guy," she said sheepishly.

Natalie shrugged. "Sort of. I mean, it's okay. He *is* cute," she added, trying to be gracious. *I mean, assuming he's still my guy and all.*

Tori squealed again—this time out of embarrassment. "Oh, my god—I am *so* sorry! That is totally uncool. And you've been so great, showing me around and stuff. I hope you're not mad."

"How could I be?" Nat asked, realizing as she said it that it was true. Tori clearly hadn't meant any harm, and she could hardly be blamed for thinking that Simon was cute. *I mean, he is,* Nat thought. *No doubt about it.*

Just looking at him sent her into fluttery spasms. She hadn't seen him since the reunion. Talking on the phone and sending e-mails just wasn't the same thing. But was it going to be, like, weird now? She had no idea. Suddenly her cheeks were buzzing, her tongue felt dry, and her hands were clammy and cold. It wasn't as though she was *so* terribly socially awkward—back home, she and Kyle Taylor had enjoyed a brief flirtation that had basically fizzled. But Nat's feelings for Simon were much stronger than any she'd ever had for Kyle Taylor, or anyone else.

"Go talk to him," Tori urged, pressing her index finger into Natalie's ribs. "He's staring at you."

Nat looked up. Simon, in fact, *did* seem to be staring at her. His eyes were practically boring holes into her forehead. *Get it together, Nat,* she willed herself.

"Go. Say. Hi." It was Alyssa, stage-whispering through clenched teeth. Thankfully, she knew Natalie all too well. Natalie took a quick glance over her shoulder and was relieved to see the full alliance of the two bunks—her friends from 4A and 4C alike—all with fingers surreptitiously crossed and well-wishing her as she step-shuffled the endless ten feet toward the pagoda.

Embarrassing as the scene with Tori had been, Nat could be grateful for the fact that Simon hadn't witnessed any of it. Thank goodness for his laid-back, easygoing attitude; he was sitting in the pagoda staring off into space, lost in his own thoughts.

"Hey," Natalie said tentatively, creeping up next to him.

Startled, Simon jumped. When he realized it was only Natalie, he relaxed and smiled. "Sorry," he said. "Very cool, right?"

"Hey, it's okay," Natalie joked, laughing. She appreciated that he wasn't the type to take himself too seriously. "It's my fault for sneaking up on you."

"That's true," he agreed. He stood and dusted off the back of his shorts. Natalie was struck by how tall he was—had a grown an extra three feet over the school year? Now she had to truly tilt her head up if she wanted to look into his eyes. Which she did. She really, really did.

Now that they were both standing, what had been a mild self-consciousness was unfolding into a massive, full-body nervous tic. Nat had no idea what to do with her hands, her fingers, her hair. She settled on tucking a stray lock of her dark hair behind one ear, crossing her arms across her chest and, finally, abandoning the stiff posture for a calculatedly breezy one-hand-on-hip, one-hand-hooked-into-back pocket pose. It seemed to work; once her arms were accounted for, she felt her body go slack as some of the tension ran off in great waves.

"So—" they both said at the same time. Nat giggled again. "You first."

"How was the rest of your year?"

Nat made a face. "Sixth grade. Homework. Fun," she said sarcastically. "But, um, my bunkmates and I kept a reading group going online. I liked that. We read some cool stuff. *The Pinballs.* Um . . . other books . . ." she finished lamely, drawing a total blank as a result of her extreme nerves.

"Oh, yeah?" Simon asked, sounding genuinely curious. "I got really into Ray Bradbury this year. I love sci-fi."

If it didn't happen in Episode III, Nat didn't know sci-fi. She was sort of limited in that genre. She smiled at Simon weakly, wondering how interested she was supposed to pretend to be. She was still fairly new at the whole dating thing. "What bunk are you in?" she asked, casually changing the subject.

"4D," Simon said. "Just across the field from you guys, right?"

"Right," she said, pleasantly surprised that he had taken the time to check out her bunk. That was definitely a good sign, shared love of sci-fi or no.

"Right," he said, glancing downward and kicking a little circle in the dust with his sneaker. Nat suddenly panicked—what if she was losing his interest? *Quick, say something*, she commanded herself. To no avail—any interesting anecdote that had happened to her within the past six months flew out of her brain, as if by magic. It was amazing, really. She couldn't think of one tiny comment to make. *My homeroom teacher would* not *believe this*, Natalie thought wryly. She was considered the class chatterbox, and small talk wasn't something that usually came difficult to her.

Maybe the awkward tension was all in her mind?

"So," Simon said, coughing slightly. "I'm going to . . ." He trailed off, gesturing mildly to where a group of boys—his bunkmates, likely—were congregated, involved in some sort of complicated spitting contest. Natalie willed herself not to shudder.

Obviously, the awkward tension was *not* all in her mind. Drat.

"Yeah, I have to—" Nat jerked her head back to where her friends stood, all furiously spying on the duo, though fervently pretending that they weren't.

"So, I'll um . . . see you later?" Simon asked, as if he wasn't sure at all that he would.

"You know where to find me," Natalie replied, instantly wondering why she had decided to be so flip. This was Simon, for Pete's sake—the boy who had held her hand and never lost his cool when they'd gotten lost last summer on a camping trip. Simon, who had e-mailed her and called her and kissed her cheek at the camp reunion. *Simon*. They were friends. Maybe more.

So why did things feel so strangely, awfully uncomfortable?

She had no idea. And she was already feeling bad about their exchange, wanting to undo some of the nerves that had spiked the air. "Look, maybe I'll come by—" she offered. Then she looked up and realized there was no point in finishing her sentence.

Simon was already gone.

Lunch was classic Lakeview cuisine: suspiciously rubbery grilled cheese sandwiches and watered-down bug juice. The mess hall was as cavernous as Nat remembered, though it was nice to see that, this year, banners from Color War the previous summer had joined the rest of the wall hangings. This way Nat could admire her own handiwork as she "ate"—or rather pushed her sandwich back and forth on her plate.

"Earth to Natalie."

Nat looked up to find Alyssa peering at her inquisitively. "What'd that poor grilled cheese ever do to you?" she teased, gesturing toward the soggy bread. "You should eat it or toss it. Put it out of its misery one way or another."

Nat shrugged. "I'm not that hungry."

"Look, it's not like I blame you," Alyssa began. "I mean, this food is toxic under the best of circumstances. But I'm your BFF and I know what's what."

"Meaning?"

Alyssa poked Natalie in the ribs. "You're annoyed because Simon didn't, like, swoop you up in some huge movie-star embrace."

Natalie rolled her eyes. "Gross. We've never

even kissed. I mean, except on the cheek. I don't think we're ready for a movie-star *embrace*."

"But still," Alyssa said, raising her eyebrows knowingly.

Natalie sighed. "Yeah, it could have gone more smoothly," she admitted. "No big-time smooch, but a little less tension would have been nice."

"So you were both a little nervous. It's normal," Alyssa said reassuringly. "I bet it will be fine once you have some time alone to talk."

"You mean some time alone to talk when I am *not* suddenly possessed by the spirit of a total spaz," Nat corrected her.

"Well, sure, you might want to work on that," Alyssa teased. "Give me a break. You were a little shy. It happens to the best of us. Even super-sophisticated city chicks, I hear."

"Ha-ha," Nat joked. Inside, though, she felt better. Alyssa always knew how to pull her out of a funk. She was so glad they were going to be spending the next two months together.

"Listen up, everybody!" It was Andie, struggling to be heard by her campers above the din. "After lunch, we're going back to the bunk to finish our unpacking. Then I'll go over the chore wheel and our daily schedule. And, of course, we'll be signing up for our first round of electives."

The girls whooped and hollered, eager to pick their free-choice activities for the first two weeks of camp. "Natalie, you're going to volunteer for nature, right?" Jenna shouted from the head of the table. She winked. Natalie, who considered herself "allergic to fresh air," had been assigned to the nature shack during the first two weeks of camp last summer. And what an initiation it had been! She had gotten lost in the woods during the group campout. The one upside to that was that she and Simon had gotten lost together—which was when they had broken down and admitted their feelings for each other. *So, it was actually a pretty happy ending,* she admitted to herself.

"Hey, it worked out pretty well for me last summer," Natalie quipped. "No complaints here."

"Ugh, if you're leading the overnight, count me out," Chelsea chimed in snidely. "I mean, you're hardly a Girl Scout."

Natalie chose to ignore the nasty blonde. "Whatever, Chelse," she said dismissively. "I'm psyched for free choice—no matter what I get." She eyed Andie slyly. "Though I wouldn't, you know, *hate* it if I got arts and crafts, and newspaper."

"We'll see what I can do," Andie replied, smiling.

Natalie turned to Tori eagerly. "You *have* to sign up for newspaper," she said. "Since you're from L.A. you'll be *perfect* to cowrite the mock 'gossip column.' I mean, it's gossip, but nothing, you know, mean-spirited. Alyssa used to do it with me, but she considers it a compromise of her artistic integrity. So I, for one, am especially glad that you're here."

Alyssa shrugged innocently. "Take my byline, please. This summer I'm determined to learn how to take a decent picture, anyway."

"Sure, maybe," Tori said. "I love to write. I'll

mention that to Andie." She frowned. "I'm all unpacked," she said. "What do we do while everyone gets assigned their chores and stuff?"

"Oooh," Natalie said, a gleam in her eye. "I have the perfect way to pass time!"

"Makeovers?" Jessie asked, squealing in excitement. She whirled to Lauren and Anna, who sat on either side of her. "Nat gives the *best* makeovers! She's like a pro at manicures."

Natalie nodded proudly. "*And* I have the most *amazing* new eyeshadow kit from St—"

"Wait, the one with khaki shadow-creams?" Tori interrupted, eager.

"No," Nat admitted, shaking her head. "I, um, haven't seen that one yet."

"You *haven't?*" Tori shrieked. "Poor, deprived child! I'll tell my mom to mail mine up tomorrow. That way, we can all bask in the glory of the shadow-cream. Thank goodness, in the meantime I have the super-slick lip tint to tide us over."

"I've actually been wanting to try that," Perry said.

The other girls nodded in agreement, murmuring excitedly. Even Alyssa seemed super-enthusiastic about lip tint, which for her was somewhat unusual. Alyssa's fashion and grooming tastes tended to run more toward the artsy side.

There it was again—that slightly edgy sensation. But what was it all about? Was Natalie actually annoyed that Alyssa and Tori seemed to be getting along? That was ridiculous.

Natalie knew it was immature to want her best friend to be more excited about her own makeup than she was about Tori's. It was nice that she and Tori had the same interests, and this way, they could all pool their resources and be ten times as fabulous as each would otherwise be on her own. *It's really a good thing,* she reminded herself. *Don't be a brat. I mean, it's just makeup. Who even cares, anyway?*

"I can't wait to try it," she said, trying her best to sound totally perky. Unfortunately, Tori was too busy offering beauty tips around the table—even shy, timid Karen was warming to the conversation—to appreciate Natalie's affirmation. As near as Nat could tell, just about every single camper in 4A was riveted, hanging on to Tori's every word.

Not that Natalie minded. Not at all.

▲ ▲ ▲

"How many hot dogs are you going to eat tonight at the cookout?" Alex asked. She had caught up with her friends from 4A after lunch.

Natalie shuddered. "Zero. The hot dogs here make me want to rethink the whole vegetarian thing."

"Hey, not nice!" Pete chimed in from where he was lounging by the stairs to the mess hall.

"Sorry, Pete, nothing personal," Natalie said sheepishly.

"Whatever," he sniffed, pretending to be highly offended.

"Don't mind him," Jenna teased. "He's just grouchy because Stephanie didn't come back this year."

Jenna's older sister, Stephanie, had been a CIT the previous summer, and she and Pete had had a "thing."

"That's true," he said agreeably. "So don't go insulting my hot dogs. My fragile ego can't take it."

"Fine, so I'll eat, like, sixty hot dogs," Alyssa offered. The other girls cracked up. Alyssa didn't eat meat, even under the best of circumstances.

"Look, Pete—the power of your cooking has inspired Alyssa to abandon her principles." Grace smiled wickedly.

"We can't get into this now," Natalie said to her friends. "We have to get back to the bunk. There's that whole free-choice thing to deal with. I mean, even if I don't get nature, I could get stuck with sports!"

Jenna cracked up. "That'd be awesome. You in soccer with Alex and me."

"No way," Nat said. "You guys would kill me."

"Soccer, Nat?"

Natalie looked up and almost tripped, she was so surprised. It was Simon again, smiling down at her. "You *have* to be kidding. No way the Natalie *I* know would be voluntarily signing up for sports and nature."

"Hey," Nat protested, feeling bolder now that she had regained her footing. "Nature wasn't *all* bad." She smiled at him.

"You're right," he conceded. "But I have a better idea for this summer. How about we both sign up for newspaper instead?"

Nat had to forcibly restrain herself from jumping out of her skin with excitement. Simon wanted to plan their free choice together? This was big. This was, like, a whole new level for them. She somehow managed to muster up enough composure to nod. She didn't trust herself with actual words. Simon nodded back and disappeared off with his friends.

Dimly, in the periphery of her consciousness, Natalie could hear her friends shrieking and catcalling, hollering and making loud, smacking kissing noises. She knew she'd be teased about her little newspaper plans for at least the rest of the afternoon. At *least*.

The funny thing was, she didn't mind at all.

chapter FOUR

"Uuuughhhh . . . I am never, ever eating another hot dog for as long as I live," Jenna moaned, clutching her stomach.

"Or at least until the next cookout," Karen quipped. Karen was making lots more jokes and comments than she had the year before, Natalie noticed. It was nice to see her coming out of her shell. She was chattering away on her way back to the bunk after dinner.

"Maybe the trick is to eat *one* hot dog instead of *seven*," Chelsea suggested, her voice oozing with faux-helpfulness. Jenna was smart enough to ignore her, instead sipping gingerly at a can of soda.

"So, no icebreakers?" Natalie said, turning to Andie inquisitively. "No 'I'm Going on a Picnic,' trust falls, weird riddles about locked rooms and sealed windows?" It was exciting, she realized, to be among people who (mostly) knew all of her secrets—unlike last summer, she had nothing to hide. What a relief! Last year, the prospect of icebreakers—and having to lie about things like her father's job—had terrified her. Now, everything was different. *Bring on the icebreakers*, she decided. *I'm an open book!*

The cookout had been great—food notwith-standing—and a nice chance for the 4A-ers to see their friends in 4C and mingle with others in the division. But Natalie knew the real fun would be in bonding with her bunkmates back at home base, back at the bunk itself. And the first night was the night when after-hours giggles, storytelling, and even contraband snacks were most likely to be overlooked by Andie and Mia.

"You read my mind, Nat," Andie said. "Why don't we all get comfortable?" She patted the wooden floor and settled herself Indian-style. "Mia, do you have the, um, supplies?" she asked meaningfully.

"Sure do!" Mia chirped, diving into her cubby and emerging, moments later, with a huge bag of marshmallows, a package of chocolate chip cookies, and the biggest bag of M&M's that Natalie had ever seen. "Dig in, guys!" she said, opening up the packages and passing them around.

The bunkmates wasted no time in assembling themselves in a circle and obliging, tearing into the treats as though they hadn't just come from a huge barbecue. When the cookies found Jenna, she stared at the box, peered into it, closed the cardboard flaps, and passed the box along.

A moment later, she grabbed the box back. "What the heck. I'm already dying as it is," she said, shrugging and shoveling a cookie into her mouth.

"Did everyone get the M&M's?" Andie asked.

The girls chorused their affirmation.

"Great," Andie said. "Don't eat them."

"Huh?" they whined in unison.

"Yet," Andie amended hastily. "Don't eat them yet." She glanced around the circle. "We're all here, yes?" She did a quick head count. "And we all have M&M's. Great." She held out her hand to show the girls her own collection—a modest fist of candy. "Six," she said. "So that means that I get to tell you six things about me."

Another wave of hushed conversation erupted among the bunkmates as they all deftly reassessed their candy collections. Nat realized with relief that she had stocked up on cookies to the exclusion of much of anything else. Alyssa, however, had not fared as well. *Sucker.* She'd be regaling her bunkmates with every anecdote she could muster from the time she'd taken her first step until the minute she stepped off the bus that afternoon.

Andie cleared her throat. "You get the gist of the game. We thought the candy would make for a nice bribe. So, anyway, I'll start. As you know, I'm Andie, and this is my first summer as a counselor at Lakeview. Before this summer I worked as a CIT at Camp Arrowhead, which is in upstate New York. I went there as a camper for five years before that." She ticked off the facts in her head, nodding to herself. "Three more. Okay, well, I have a boyfriend, Brad, who is traveling in Tahoe this summer. I totally miss him"—the girls giggled at this admission—"and maybe he'll come up for Visiting Day." The girls squealed with delight. "Done," Andie said with finality.

"Hey, no fair. Two of those points were about Brad, not you," Jenna protested.

"Do you really want to go there, Jenna?" Andie teased, nodding her head toward Jenna's handful of candy.

"Point taken," Jenna said, smiling sheepishly. "Thank you for sharing."

The girls went around the circle systematically occasionally sneaking bites of their stashes and thereby rendering the game slightly more manageable. Natalie learned that Chelsea's favorite color was purple, and that she liked to eat peanut butter and jelly sandwiches that had been grilled first, which was kind of an interesting idea and not something that would have ever occurred to Natalie. Alyssa kept every single piece of artwork she'd ever created, even notebook doodlings. "My mom is dying to clean out my closet," she confessed. She got around her massive heap of candy by naming each and every masterpiece individually.

Karen shocked them all by explaining that she had given away her stuffed animal collection to a homeless shelter in her hometown. "I think it was time," she said. Natalie and the others rushed to protest, not wanting her to feel bad about her hobby.

"You gave them *all* away?" Jessie asked, wide-eyed. It was, after all, a lot of stuffed animals.

"Almost all," Karen admitted shyly, causing them all to break out in laughter again.

"Well, each one of these M&M's counts for every member of my family," Jenna announced, before popping six of them in her mouth at one time. "And, as some of you know, I have a twin brother. He's here, too." She gobbled two more. "My parents got divorced last summer, which was yucky at first, but now I'm sort of used to it and it's kind of fun to have two of everything . . ." She paused thoughtfully, then chomped down on three more pieces of candy. "I rock at soccer, you'll see," she told the newcomers, "*and* I'm really modest about it." She winked. Then she cocked her head in Andie's direction again. "Do I really have to come up with"—she glanced down at her hand in despair—"I can't even count how many." She brightened. "What if they melted together and made one big hunk of chocolate?"

Andie shook her head ruefully. "One more factoid, dearie, and we'll move on."

"Um, well, unlike some of my bunkmates, I am *totally* not into boys," Jenna said defiantly. "Done!" She popped the rest of the chocolate into her mouth all at once. "Yum!" Everyone laughed.

Jessie got off easy. "Allergic to chocolate," she explained. "But, um, I'm really into sports, too. Not soccer. I mean, it's okay, but at home I play field hockey, and I love to Rollerblade." Her curly, brunette ponytail bobbed up and down as she spoke.

Lauren was born on a leap year. Perry had a golden retriever puppy that her parents had adopted when she'd gotten an A in reading. Anna was relieved to be away from her four-year-old sister for two whole months. ("She's cute, but the built-in babysitter thing gets old.") Mia, like Jenna, had a twin, though hers was an identical twin, who was doing a high-school exchange program in Australia over the summer. "So she won't be coming up for Visiting Day," Mia said sadly. "I totally miss her."

Finally it was Natalie's turn. "Well, I'm really excited to be back here for another summer," she giggled. "I chose to come back myself—can you believe it?" She turned to Andie. "I wasn't exactly a Girl Scout my first summer here. Anyway, that's two things, right?" Andie nodded. "And, um, my mom is away, doing more art buying this summer in Europe, and my dad and his girlfriend are buying a new house. It's in the Hollywood Hills, near when Brad and Jen used to live." She loved that little detail, even though she knew that by the time her dad and Josie moved in, they'd have a whole new set of neighbors. "As some of you know, my dad is an actor. Tad Maxwell."

Most of the campers knew this already, so they took it in stride. And the others were managing not to have any sort of weird reactions. Nat had to marvel at how cool everyone was being. And just this time last year she was so worried to tell them the truth about her parents!

"That's crazy that your dad is Tad Maxwell! I *love* his movies! And that he's moving in next door to Brad and Jen's house—my mom says that Jennifer has the *best* stylist in L.A.!" Tori gushed. "She gets featured in every magazine, and she's never on the fashion 'don'ts' list." She stopped herself abruptly, realizing that she had cut Natalie off. "Omigosh, I am *so* rude. I didn't mean to interrupt you, Natalie. I just get excited talking celebrity-stalking, you know?"

"Totally," Nat said. "My dad's girlfriend and I love to have lunch at the Ivy—"

"The *Ivy!*" Tori shrieked. "I *totally* sat next to Tom and Katie there!" She turned to Andie breathlessly. "Does that count as three things for me?"

Andie smiled. "The game has pretty much broken down, anyway. What do you say we dispense with the formalities?"

The girls were more than happy to oblige. They hit the snacks with renewed abandon, glad to be able to chat more free-form. "How tall is Tom in real life?" Jessie asked, sidling up closer to Tori on the floor.

"And, um, what's her *real* hair color?" Perry chimed in.

Nat looked down. She still had a rainbow of brightly colored candy resting in her cupped palm. But no one was paying any attention to the game anymore. *Guess I'm off the hook,* she thought. Tori had distracted them all when she started in like a deranged gossip columnist.

She popped the chocolate in her mouth and chewed thoughtfully. *Lucky me.*

"Yeah, *Natalie!!!* Woo-hoo!"

Nat could hear Jenna, Jessie, and the rest of her teammates screeching at the top of their lungs as she flew around the bases. *First, second, third . . .* she thought, the breath rising up in her chest rapidly. *Keep going.*

She was—she could hardly believe it—

rounding home plate! In her whole life, Nat had never won a round of sudden-death kickball, and she herself had never kicked a homerun. This was . . . this was *amazing*. Camp was *way* awesome the second time around!

She sprinted home, taking care to tap the plate as she sped past it.

"Did I make it?" she gasped, grinning and wiping the sweat off of her forehead with the back of her hand.

"I'll say!" Alyssa exclaimed, whistling in admiration. "Who are you, and what have you done with Natalie?"

Natalie shrugged modestly. "I know, I know, it's incredible. It's all about focus and energy," she said, sounding like one of those motivational athletes you always saw on TV just after she'd won an Olympic medal or whatever.

"Seriously, Natalie—it *is* incredible," Eric, the new sports counselor, chimed in. "I mean, aren't you the girl who would duck every time the ball came near her last summer?"

"Yup," Chelsea snapped. "Looks like she finally managed to get the basics down. Only a year too late. Impressive. *Not.*"

"Whatever, Natalie, we're totally impressed," Lauren said, waving her hand at Chelsea dismissively. "I can't remember the last time I had a homerun."

"Not during this game," Chelsea said. "And, anyway, while you were all fawning over Natalie, Anna struck out. We're in the field."

The girls took their positions as 4B came off the field and up to bat. A few of them clapped Natalie on the back as they passed by, saying, "nice one," or "awesome job." Natalie wasn't used to getting praised for her sports skills. She understood, finally, why Jenna and Alex would get so amped about soccer matches. A girl could get used to being MVP.

"What's my position again?" Tori asked, looking confused. "God, I am, like, allergic to sports. I take Pilates with my mother—that's *it*. And once a month we go on a twenty-four-hour juice fast. It's totally the latest thing in L.A."

Natalie clucked her tongue sympathetically. She wasn't into any crazy fitness trends—a juice fast sounded completely gross—but she knew what it was like to be totally sports-averse. "Trust me, I understand. At home I am either Rollerblading with my best friend in the park, or I'm camped out in front of the TiVo. No organized sports for *moi*. We're outfield, remember? It's nice and easy. If and when a ball even makes it out here, chances are, someone will go for it before we do. And even if no one does, we've got plenty of time to brace ourselves."

Tori smiled gratefully. "Sounds perfect." She frowned. "How close am I allowed to stand to you?"

Natalie laughed. "You're fine where you are."

"Right, right," Tori said, nodding. "We want to look like we're trying, huh?"

Nat nodded her head, giggling. "Definitely." As she said it, though, she felt a trickle of sweat run down the back of her leg, no doubt left over from her spontaneous burst of major-league talent. Suddenly, she wasn't sure if she just wanted to *look* like she was trying, or if she wanted to actually try. Trying had been. . . kind of fun. More than kind of.

"Who's up?" Tori asked, squinting into the sun.

"Um . . . it looks like . . . Lainie is up?" Natalie guessed, as a petite girl with white-blond hair stepped up to the plate. "I have no idea whether she's any good or not. Brace yourself."

Lainie yanked on the ends of her ponytail, tightening it, and prepped for the pitch. She was normally a bubbly and vivacious girl, but she took this game very seriously, and her usually easygoing expression was currently replaced by one of sheer determination.

Jessie stepped up to the pitcher's mound with an equally fierce look. She leaned forward and rolled the kickball with perfect precision. Natalie tensed; obviously she wasn't exactly an expert on the subject, but judging from Lainie's posture . . . she was going to kick the ball at a certain angle . . . and it would probably travel . . . in a particular direction . . .

Slam! The ball came soaring toward Natalie, who raised the flat of her hand up to her forehead to shield the sun from her eyes. *Here we go*, she thought. She knew she could catch the ball if she could line herself up with its trajectory. "I got it," she said, stepping backward and outstretching her arms. "I got it!"

The ball sailed toward her in a perfect arc. It landed forcefully, the rubber edging scraping against her fingernails. *I'll need to file those again later*, Natalie thought wildly. "I've got—"

"She's got it!" Tori shrieked, running toward Nat.

Which was when it happened.

It was like a bad dream, like a movie set to slow-motion. One minute, Natalie was hugging the kickball to her stomach like precious cargo, and the next second, Tori, who up until now had been loudly cheering from a peanut-gallery perch three steps or so away, was hurdling toward her . . .

And then she tripped.

Tori tripped on a rock, or a twig, or some other form of . . . *nature* . . . strewn across the field, and stumbled forward.

Directly into Natalie, to be precise. Natalie yelped and staggered backward, dropping the ball.

"SAFE!" Eric called, extending his arms out in front of him in a gesture that Nat assumed meant the same. She wasn't sure; she could barely see from her position flat on her back with Tori tangled up in front of her.

"Safe?" she repeated, sputtering a little bit.

"Yeah." It was Jenna's voice, coming from somewhere above her. "Sorry, Nat, that was a good catch. You tried. I'm impressed."

"Thanks," Natalie said as someone—probably Jenna—pulled Tori off of her. "Ooof. Not that it helped anything."

"It was amazing, though, seriously," Jenna said. "I love this new team spirit thing you're working. If you keep this up, you're going to get the MVP award at our end-of-camp banquet."

"Yeah, I'll, um, hold off on telling my mom to clear a place on the mantel," Natalie joked, standing gingerly and dusting the grass off of herself. "God, I'm a mess."

"You're fine," Tori said, leaning forward and picking a blade of grass out of Natalie's hair. "Well, now you are." She frowned, peering down at her fingers. "I, on the other hand, broke a nail. Darn it." She shrugged. "Well, I guess sports aren't my thing." She giggled to herself and wandered off, apparently completely unconcerned with the fact that Lissy, another 4B-er, was stepping up to the plate to kick.

That's just it, Natalie thought, frustrated. *Sports aren't my thing, either.* At least, they weren't before this morning. And it looked like they wouldn't be anytime soon—again today, anyway. Not that Nat cared.

Or did she?

▲ ▲ ▲

By lunchtime, all thoughts of her fall from athletic grace were gone from Natalie's mind. She had seen Simon at the waterfront, and he'd told her he would stop by during the siesta period after lunch. Now Nat's biggest concern was how she was going to scribble a postcard to Hannah before he showed up.

"What did one snowman say to the other snowman?" Perry asked as the girls kicked along the dirt path that ran from the bunks to the mess hall.

Natalie looked at Alyssa and shrugged. "We

have no idea," Alyssa said.

"Freeze!" Perry screamed, adopting a Charlie's Angels pose and laughing maniacally.

"Very mature," Chelsea sniffed.

Nat smiled. Okay, it was a stupid joke, but whatever. At least Perry was always upbeat and energetic—which was more than anyone could say for Chelsea.

"Hey, aren't those your friends from last summer?" Tori asked, pointing.

Natalie and Alyssa looked off into the distance, where Tori was pointing. Indeed, Alex, Brynn, Valerie, Sarah, and Grace were marching together in a Rockettes-style kick line, chanting. Natalie opened her mouth to say hi to her friends but realized they were too involved in their chant to hear her. As they drew closer, the words to their little cheer became clearer:

"Hey, 4A: Save your toilet paper 'cause we're going to wipe you up!"

They'd clap heartily through linked arms after each rendition, growing progressively louder.

"Whaaaaaa?" Jenna murmured incredulously, almost more to herself than to anyone else. "That's crazy!"

"People are starting to notice what they're saying," Jessie said nervously, tugging at the tips of her pigtails. Inter-bunk rivalries were not uncommon and generally were all in good fun—but as other campers started to ogle the two sparring bunks, Natalie and her friends flushed with embarrassment.

"All right, kids, break it up," Andie shouted,

waving her arms like a particularly friendly train conductor. 4C acquiesced, but only after a minute or two more of stubborn catcalls and hollers. "Does this happen at Lakeview often?" Andie asked her campers, bemused.

Jenna nodded. "Oh, yeah. You know, rivalries. I think they're starting up because half of our old bunk is in 4A, and half is in 4C. So it's like, us against them. And 4C is going to have to pay."

Andie smiled mischievously. "I like the sound of that," she said. "A lot."

chapter FIVE

It took only a few days for Natalie to find her feet and truly settle into the camp routine. Every morning, the girls were woken at the crack of oh-my-god, and were given twenty minutes to get down to flag raising. That was twenty minutes total, for the collective group, as Nat had learned the hard way the summer before. She was extremely proud of herself for having considerably pared down her a.m. regimen. A quick shower, a tug of the hairbrush, and she was done.

At flag raising, the entire camp did just that, with Dr. Steve, the camp director, leading them all in calisthenics and a few cheesy songs. He also made announcements, if there were any to be made. Then it was time for breakfast—or what passed for breakfast, anyway. After breakfast, all of the campers returned to their respective bunks for chores. They then traveled as a bunk to sports and instructional swim, broke up for electives, met for a specialty (sports, art, wood-working, photography, ceramics, newspaper, or nature), and then had lunch. After lunch was siesta, where they were free to do as they pleased as long as they remained in or near the bunk and were quiet enough to give their counselors a break. After siesta came another bunk activity, free swim, and then finally, their last elective. They had some more free time before dinner, followed by evening activity. It was amazing how leisure activities could fill up a whole day so quickly.

Natalie was thrilled to be assigned to ceramics and newspaper for her free choices, both of which she got to do with Alyssa. As he had said he would, Simon had signed up for newspaper, too. Nat felt deliriously lucky—her BFF and her boyfriend—both in her elective! Newspaper was fast becoming her favorite activity of the day.

Today, though, she was feeling antsy. It felt like Jesse, the new newspaper counselor, had been talking at them, rather than to them, for hours, rather than minutes.

"Well, we've talked about how to write a catchy, captivating headline," Jesse said. "You guys know that you have exactly three seconds to get your reader's attention. So you have to be concise and punchy. It's not easy to do. But that being said, a catchy headline is only as good as the article it . . . well, headlines."

Nat rolled her eyes. Could you say *obvious?* Jesse sure wasn't being very catchy or to-the-point. Next to her, Alyssa giggled. *Probably thinking the same thing I am,* Nat decided.

"Today we're going to talk about interviews," Jesse continued. If he noticed Nat and Alyssa's little psychic side conversation, he was being nice enough not to call attention to it. "Interviews can range from anything like celebrity gossip, like Oprah and Jen, to hard-hitting news, like, oh, almost anything Mike Wallace does on *60 Minutes*."

"*Booorrrr-ing*," trilled one of the more obnoxious boys from the back row. Why he was even in newspaper, Nat had no idea. Maybe he'd been stuck with it, like she had with nature the summer before. The memory still made her cringe—but at least it had brought her and Simon together. *The Great Outdoors is good for something—who knew?*

"Yes, well, obviously you're entitled to your opinion, and of course, it's all a matter of taste. But still." He gestured to the long wooden table before him. "I have a bunch of samples here. *Spin, Twist, Jane, Entertainment Weekly, Time, Sports Illustrated*—"

"—Woo-hoo!" Obnoxious and his friends chimed in. Nat rolled her eyes. Boys were so predictable. Thank goodness Simon could be counted on to be a tad more . . . couth.

"You can take some time researching, and then pair up. I want you to work on interviewing each other. Whoever is best able to come up with a compelling interview will be asked to submit a piece—an interview—to the Visiting Day edition of our paper."

A small murmur of excitement rippled across the room. The newspaper came out twice over the summer—Visiting Day, and at the end-of-camp banquet. The Visiting Day paper was considered a bigger deal, though, because of how many parents were around to read it.

When no one moved, Jesse looked at them all quizzically. "You can take some time researching," he repeated. "Pair up." When no one moved, he clarified. "Now. Would be fine."

The campers cracked up, then one by one shifted out of their benches and wandered semi-aimlessly through the newspaper office/shack, occasionally flipping through the samples that Jesse had laid out but mostly stealing sidelong glances at one another. Obnoxious easily found a partner—no doubt someone just as loud as himself, Nat decided—and some of the girls squealed quietly and ran toward each other, as well.

"So are you gonna Barbara Walters me or what?"

Natalie looked up to find Simon grinning at her. Immediately, her pulse quickened and her temperature shot up at least five degrees. He'd been sitting a few seats away and she had hoped, hoped, hoped he would come over and ask to be partners. "You know Barbara Walters has a habit of getting to the core of the issue," Natalie warned, waving her index finger reprovingly. "I think she considers it a personal failure if she can't get her guest to burst into tears onscreen."

She tapped her chin with her forefinger thoughtfully. "Oprah, Mike Wallace, Barbara Walters," she recited. "Doesn't anyone *read* the news anymore?"

"Is that the resounding yes I was looking for?"

Nat giggled and nodded shyly. "Yeah, I was thinking we could do at least one of the interviews in the style of a tabloid. You know, really trashy and pulpy."

Simon nodded. "Ah, high-quality. Maybe I'll finally be granted that ever-elusive Pulitzer?"

"Forget the Pulitzers! I'm thinking the *Post*. Sleazier. *Hello!* You know, like the British gossip rags," Alyssa said, sidling up to Nat. "What do you say, partner?"

The look on Alyssa's face was expectant and earnest, and Natalie realized with a sinking feeling that her friend expected them to be buddies. And why wouldn't she? They always had been before. Wasn't that why they had signed up for newspaper together in the first place?

Nat glanced a little bit desperately at Simon, who in turn simply coughed and stared off at an imaginary point in the distance. *Coward.* Nat was on her own.

"Oh, ah . . ." Natalie stammered, feeling awkward. "I just . . . it's just that I . . ."

Alyssa's gaze traveled from Natalie's mortified, guilty expression to Simon's avoidant stare, and back to Natalie again. Her posture went rigid as she realized her mistake. "Oh, I got it," she said. "Never mind."

"No, but—" Natalie said, panicking but not sure what she could really say or do. "Maybe we could triple up?"

Alyssa peered at her friend. "Nat," she said sternly. "There are plenty of people in this elective with us. I will find someone else. Do not sweat it."

Relief flooded Natalie's veins. She adored

Alyssa, of course, and would have had an amazing time working with her. But she seriously couldn't pass up the opportunity to partner with Simon. It was just so . . . girlfriendly. In a good way.

Besides, she reasoned to herself, *he asked you first, didn't he?*

Sure, it was a rationalization. But it worked.

"Horoscope, please."

"Cancer . . ." Nat scanned her magazine to find Alyssa's daily dose of "woo woo advice," as she liked to call it. She loved that her friend indulged her obsession with astrology even though she totally didn't believe in it. That was real dedication.

The day after the little interview awkwardness, the two were sitting out free swim, as usual. Another tic of Natalie's of which Alyssa was uber-tolerant; Nat was a great swimmer but hated to go in the lake. It was just so . . . gloppy and cloudy and non-chlorinated. Who knew what sorts of things were swimming around in there? Yak. The slight weirdness of newspaper was long forgotten, Alyssa being hard at work on a *Rolling Stone*-esque piece with a goth girl who was also in newspaper and Nat studiously perusing *Star* and *Hello!* for inspiration for her interview with Simon. Nat and Alyssa were both so hard at work that their respective notebooks, notes, and first drafts were tossed aside in favor of the fashion magazine that Nat was now brandishing.

"Hmm . . . Cancer . . ." she scanned the page.

Alyssa was a water sign; it was no wonder she was so creative. "You . . . uh-oh . . ." she said, trailing off abruptly.

"What?" Alyssa asked, raising one eyebrow with alarm. "You must spill."

"It says . . ." Nat stopped again. She looked at Alyssa with a gleam in her eye. "It says to beware of wet bunkmates."

"Huh?" Alyssa asked. Before she could figure out what was going on, she was hit with a sudden shower of water. "Wha???" she cried, jumping up. She turned around to find Jenna grinning madly at her, fresh from the lake and dripping wet.

Jenna winked. "Gotcha." She smiled. "Sorry." She didn't sound sorry at all.

Alyssa groaned and grabbed at Jenna's towel, drying herself off good-naturedly. Soon the rest of their bunkmates emerged from the water, teeth chattering and ponytails drenched. Mia was off setting up for lunch, but Andie, who'd been pinch-hitting for a sick lifeguard, rounded the girls up. "Time to get back to the bunk and change! Who's hungry?" she called, clapping her hands together.

"Hungry, yes, but not for camp food," Anna said. Even though she was new, it hadn't taken her very long to learn the score.

"Seriously, by the end of the summer, I'm going to be falling out of my clothes," Tori chimed in.

"Hey," Jenna said, changing the subject. "It's Grace! Grace!" she called to her friend. "Do you want to come over during siesta? We're going to play cards!"

In response, Grace shook her red curls emphatically. "I can't consort with the enemy," she teased. She linked arms possessively with Alex. Brynn and Val trailed behind, also with their noses in the air. They hummed to the beat of their "save your toilet paper" cheer as they marched by.

"Unbelievable," Jenna said as the girls disappeared out of earshot. She shook her head as if to underscore her complete and total lack of belief. Just one year ago, the girls from 4A and 4C had been united as partners in crime, and just about all else.

Natalie shrugged. "We were split up. What are you going to do? We might as well make a 'thing' about it." Nat wasn't above a little bit of drama now and then. She *was* Tad Maxwell's daughter, after all.

"A 'thing,'" Chelsea muttered. "Gosh, Nat, you're always so articulate."

"No, I get what you mean," Jenna said. Her eyes were taking on a devious sparkle.

Nat shook her head. "Jenna." She didn't say anything more. She didn't think she had to—Jenna's love of mischief had gotten her into more than enough trouble the summer before.

"Do I sense a plan hatching?" Tori asked, her voice taking on a coaxing lilt. "My mom said her favorite memories of her time at Lakeview were the pranks she and her friends pulled on each other."

"Your mother's a wise woman," Jenna said. The rest of the bunkmates, including the newbies, exchanged worried glances. "Very wise."

Tori giggled. "What did you have in mind?"

Alyssa shook her head in disapproval. "Not a good idea to encourage her."

"Aw, come on Alyss," Jenna said. "Just a little bit of fun, I promise."

"No such thing," Alyssa said, but it was obvious her resolve was starting to crack.

"No harm, no foul."

"At least tell us, for Pete's sake," Chelsea snapped, her patience wearing thin. "Jeez."

"That's what I like to hear," Jenna said, wrapping her towel around her lower half, sarong-style, and stepping into her flip-flops. She rubbed her hands together conspiratorially. "I have a few thoughts—just off the top of my head, off course . . ." She grabbed her swim tag and goggles and started off in the direction of the bunk, the rest of 4A hot on her trail.

Natalie and Alyssa met each other's eyes, each wondering just what can of worms they had opened. No harm, no foul, sure—and camp was definitely all about playful rivalries, but . . . Natalie wasn't above a *little* bit of drama.

If only she could be sure that a little bit of drama was all that Jenna had in store.

"Oh! Um, 'Pink Cadillac'!" Nat shouted out.

"No dice," Alyssa said. "Sarah already suggested that one, remember?"

Evening activity was a singdown, followed by some s'mores. This combo was one of Nat's favorites, seeing as how it didn't involve a whole lot of athleticism and it *did* involve chocolate. Good times. Singdown was fun. The campers were broken up into two teams—in this case, boys against girls—and given different topics, like "colors" or "cars." The challenge was to come up with as many songs that mention the particular category as possible. The teams took turns singing songs from their list, and the team with the most songs won. But if the opposing team took one of your songs before you did, they got the point. Right now, Andie, Mia, and Farrah, a counselor from 4B, were trying to make sense of the cacophony of song titles being screamed at them all at once. The category was "colors," and the girls·had a ton of suggestions.

"'Yellow Submarine,'" Alyssa called. "My dad loves the Beatles," she explained to her friends.

"Mine too," Tori said enthusiastically. "Paul McCartney was looking for new representation a few years back and I think my dad had high hopes, but it didn't work out."

"Did someone already say, 'It's Not Easy Being Green'?" Karen asked in her usual quiet voice.

"You *would* use the freakin' Muppets!" Chelsea hooted. "You're such a baby." She rolled her eyes. "But, no, it hasn't been called yet."

"If it hasn't been called yet, it's good," Nat said, coming to her friend's defense.

"'Blue Velvet,'" Brynn shrieked, her high-pitched voice nearly piercing Natalie's eardrums. She and Alex high-fived each other, and Natalie had to laugh. It was really nice, she conceded, to be working with her friends in this activity. Camp was great, but weird, with the core group from 3C broken up. Nat was savoring the sense of unity.

Especially since, after what Jenna had in mind for 4C, she wasn't totally sure they'd all be friends again anytime soon.

"'Black or White,'" Val offered, striking a Michael Jackson esque pose.

A loud whistle blew, signifying the end of the brainstorming session. Susan, head counselor of the Fourth Division, stepped before the roaring bonfire. "Since the boys went first last time, the girls will go first this time."

Andie gestured to the girls, who were waiting eagerly. "'Black or White,'" she mouthed deliberately. She counted down on her fingers, "One, two . . ."

On "three," the girls jumped in with thunderous energy. Hearing the first line of their song, the boys reacted with frustrated scowls, causing the girls to howl with laugher and sing even louder. It was a double bonus to know that they were gaining the point and *also* taking one out from under the guys.

The singdown went on for a while, the girls winning one round, the boys winning another, and the girls coming out on top in a sudden death round. As the girls were declared the victors, Nat realized her throat was so hoarse that she could barely cheer.

"What's our prize?" Tori asked, clapping her hands and whistling good-naturedly.

"Good stuff," Natalie explained. "We'll get the

s'mores fixings before the boys do. And if we take our time, we can *really* prolong their agony."

"I like the way you think, Manhattan," Tori said.

"We chicks have to stick together," Natalie said agreeably, holding her hand out for a skewer that Alyssa was proffering. "See?" she added, indicating the skewer. "Teamwork."

"I also grabbed us some extra marshmallows," Alyssa said, holding out her cupped palm so the girls could see her contraband goodies. "Shh."

Natalie nodded approvingly. "Well done."

"I think the thing to do is to pocket them for the time being," Alyssa said, "if you can stash them in your pocket without getting them squishy or linty."

"Check. No lint," Tori said. "And my sweatshirt has *really* big pockets."

Nat speared a marshmallow onto her skewer as Tori and Alyssa did the same. Sufficiently equipped, the three made their way closer to the fire.

"Hey, Nat." Natalie felt a tug on her arm. It was Simon.

"Hey," she said, instantly breaking into a warm grin.

"So much for chicks sticking together," Tori joked.

"I was just thinking that," Alyssa agreed.

"I got you something," he said. He lowered his voice. "But, uh, you have to be cool." He glanced sideways in either direction.

"Aren't I always?" Natalie asked, playful.

He shook the sleeve of his long-sleeved T-shirt and out slid a Hershey's Cookies and Cream bar. Nat's eyes widened. "White chocolate! My favorite!" she exclaimed. "How did you . . ."

He nodded knowingly. "I could never forget something like a person's favorite type of candy. And you should know . . . there's more where that came from."

Nat laughed. She knew he must have brought up a few bars just for her. The thought sent a little thrill down her spine. Now she and Simon had a little secret. *And* she had white chocolate. It was a total win-win situation.

"We could make some pretty fancy s'mores with these," Simon said, waving the candy bar tantalizingly.

"What are we waiting for?" Natalie asked. She took his free hand and led him closer to the open flame. The bonfire crackled and hissed, throwing heat outward into the cool, crisp night. Chowing down and laughing with Simon, Nat couldn't imagine a better evening.

It wasn't until she happened to glance over to see Tori and Alyssa furtively spearing their purloined marshmallows that a tiny pinch of doubt began to nag at her. It wasn't as if she had abandoned her friends for Simon, was it? Surely they understood what it was to be so much in . . . well, *like*, with a guy? She knew Alyssa would want her to have some bonding time with her boyfriend. And, besides, it wasn't like either of her friends were sitting all alone, exactly. They totally had each other. And they didn't seem to mind that, one bit. It was just . . .

Well, Nat couldn't decide whether that was a good thing, or a bad thing. But she had some idea. *You can't have it both ways*, she told herself.

But that didn't mean she couldn't *want* it both ways, did it? There was nothing wrong with wishful thinking, after all.

Natalie woke the next morning with no interest in eating breakfast. She had stuffed herself so full of s'mores at the bonfire that she couldn't imagine eating anything more for days. Or at least hours.

The hot water in the shower was sort of . . . nonexistent, so Natalie gritted her teeth and lathered up as quickly as she could. It was a grayish sort of morning, so she threw a pink hoodie over her usual tank top and denim shorts, stepped into her flip-flops, ran a brush through her hair, and flopped back down on her bed to wait for Alyssa—and now Tori, who had become integrated into the girls' routine as much as anything else.

Outside, the air was brisk and damp. It must have rained after they'd come back from the bonfire, which Nat supposed was pretty lucky. Every now and then nature threw you a break. She kept her hands stuffed into the pocket of her sweatshirt throughout the flag raising, tuning out the morning announcements.

On the way over to breakfast, Chelsea caught up with the girls. "Pretty lame about Jenna, right?" she asked.

Natalie shook her head. "What are you talking about?" Between the cold, the moist morning air, the food coma, and the post-Simon-quality-time haze, she was in a world of her own.

"Well, didn't she have something planned for 4C?" Chelsea reminded them.

"Oh, that's right!" Tori said. "I was so excited to see my first prank being pulled. My mom was nuts about pranks when she was a camper. I think she'll be disappointed if I don't have any stories for her on Visiting Day."

"Tell her not to get her hopes up," Chelsea grumbled. "Jenna's all *reformed* and whatever this summer." She managed to make the word "reformed" sound like "criminally insane" and she looked seriously annoyed.

"Jenna's parents will kill her if she gets into any more trouble this summer," Alyssa cut in. "That's probably why she hasn't really planned anything for 4C. And if you're her friend, you won't encourage her—she'll get sent home if she gets in trouble, like she did last summer. Hey, here's a thought: Why don't you pick up the slack, Chelsea?"

Chelsea rolled her eyes. "Right. 'Cause I *so* want to be the next Jenna Bloom." She sighed dramatically. "I'm going to go catch up with Karen. I need her *Seventeen* for free swim." She ran off toward the front of the group, where Karen and some others were clustered together with Andie. Mia was already at the mess hall, setting up for breakfast. Natalie did not envy the CITs their double-duty jobs.

The girls filed into the mess hall and took their seats at the long benches that served in place of chairs. Natalie flicked her bleary eyes across the table. Bug juice, burned toast, semi-melted packets of butter that sweat greasy trails out of their foil wrappers. Yum. Once the group was sitting, Mia rushed out of the kitchen carrying a large plastic platter heaped with a runny yellow substance. *Scrambled eggs*, Natalie thought. She'd pass.

Suddenly Natalie was snapped out of her morning daze by the sounds of loud, piercing shrieks. She practically flipped over backward on her bench. She— and just about everyone else in the room—snapped her head around to see what the cause for all of the hysteria was.

At first, Nat could barely locate the source of the noise. Slowly, though, she honed in on the locus of the chaos.

It was 4C's table.

Now, Natalie could make out words forming above the din. "Barf . . ." "Gross . . ." "We almost *ate* that. . . ."

Suddenly, a loud whistle resonated, quieting the room. For a breathless beat, the echo of the whistle bounced off of the walls. No one said a word. Then, Sophie's voice cracked through the tension. "They're fake."

Natalie turned to Alyssa, who shrugged her

shoulders. *Fake? What's fake?*

"I'm not eating them!" It was Gaby, the bratty girl who had been such a bully to Grace the summer before. "I don't eat eggs that have been touched by insect feet!"

"Gaby," Becky interrupted, trying to soothe the girl before she could get any more worked up. "They're plastic. Look." She took the platter of 4C's scrambled eggs and held them out to Gaby, who was scowling furiously. She pushed a heap of yellow-and-white gunk aside to reveal a nest of rubber—but realistic-looking, at least from where Natalie stood—flies.

"I don't know how those got in there," Sophie said, sounding puzzled and mildly fretful. "I'll get a new platter right away."

"Forget it," Gaby said, wrinkling her nose.

Sophie whisked back into the kitchen with the offending eggs, and slowly the tenor of the room reverted to its usual state of low-level hyperactivity. Natalie, Alyssa, and Tori were tucking into their own breakfast—no eggs, thank you—when Alex marched over from her table, a stern look fixed upon her face.

"We know it was you guys," Alex said, pointing a finger accusingly.

"I don't know what you're talking about," Alyssa said breezily. "How would we even have contaminated your breakfast, anyway? Assuming we even *wanted* to."

From her seat at the opposite side of the table, Jenna coughed loudly into her fist. "Sorry," she rasped, after her choking had subsided. "Bug juice went down the wrong pipe." She glanced away.

Oh, Jenna, Natalie thought, even though deep down she was pretty impressed by this prank. How *had* Jenna managed to get that close to 4C's breakfast, anyhow? "Yeah, *we* don't know what you're talking about," she said loyally.

"What*ever*," Alex said, clearly not buying it. "I don't eat eggs, anyway." Alex was a diabetic and very fanatical about what she put in her body. The one time she had given in to the urge to pig out, she'd gone into diabetic shock, and she wasn't about to let that happen again. She leaned in closer, practically throwing herself across the table at Jenna. "But I'll tell you this, Bloom," she said. "You'd better watch your back." She cracked a small smile, then marched back to her bunk's table.

The girls watched Alex retreat, then burst out into giggles. "Jenna, you are too much!" Tori said. "I can't wait to tell my mom about this."

"Seriously," Jenna said, her eyes wide now. "It wasn't me."

The murmurs around the table indicated that no one believed her.

Natalie turned to Chelsea, who was frowning and generally pretending to be miles above all of this immaturity. "Still think Jenna's so lame?" she teased.

To her credit, Chelsea didn't bother to dignify the comment with a response.

"Now, folks, it's really important that you brush every last speck of clay with the glaze before it goes into the kiln. If it's not totally, completely glazed, it may crack in the heat. Then you'd have to start all over again, and that's frustrating."

Natalie glanced down at the candy dish she was making. It was painted orange and black to look like a basketball, which was Simon's favorite sport. She planned to wrap it up with a mother lode of white chocolate Hershey's Kisses for him and give it to him as a surprise on the last night of camp. Which meant that it absolutely, positively could not be cracked. She surveyed the dish again, bending down to peer at it from all angles. *Better safe than sorry*, she thought, dipping her brush back into the pot of glaze and applying another liberal layer over her dish.

"I think you've got it, babe," Helene, the ceramics instructor, told her gently. "Another coat and you'll tip the whole clay-to-glaze ratio way out of balance."

"Right. Done," Nat said, resting her brush on the newspaper-covered table and stepping backward away from her work. "Finished."

"Looks good," Alyssa called to her.

"Not as awesome as yours," Nat said earnestly. Her friend was creating a very elaborate flowerpot thing with a Jackson Pollock motif. *Only Alyssa*, Natalie thought.

"Seriously," Tori broke in, looking up from her simple coffee mug. "There's a boutique on Melrose that sells that sort of stuff, like funky housewares and whatever. You could totally sell your vase there. It's that good."

"Aw, shucks, you girls," Alyssa said, blushing a little bit. Natalie knew that her friend had total confidence in her amazing artistic abilities but didn't really like being the center of attention.

"We can say we knew you when," Natalie joked.

"No, I'm not kidding. My mom's friend owns the shop—Astrid Landon? You know, that model? My dad does her contracts, and that's how she became friends with my mom."

"You know Astrid Landon?" Given that her father was pretty much a megastar, Natalie didn't usually get weird or celebrity-struck. But Astrid Landon was a different story. Astrid Landon was, like, her father's arch-nemesis.

Her father tried to be discrete about these things, but Nat had gotten the story out of him over one Fourth of July weekend several years ago. Tad's long-time girlfriend, Josie McLaughlan, had been on the short list to play against him in one of the *Spy* sequels, but at the last minute, Astrid's agent had pulled some strings. . . . Josie was a good sport, of course, but she'd been terribly hurt. In the long run, the movie had done modestly at the box office and the whole incident was forgotten, but Tad had sworn he wouldn't work with Astrid again. And now Tori's family was, like, best friends with her?

That wasn't something Nat could hold against Tori. *Was* it?

No, those sorts of things happened in Hollywood

all the time, Natalie knew. It wasn't Tori's fault she was on the wrong side of a celebrity-feud. It was just . . . annoying.

"Yeah, she's great," Tori gushed. "I wish they would let us keep our cell phones up here. I'd take a picture of that vase so I could show it to Astrid when I get back home."

"I know. When I first got here last summer and they took our phones away, I thought I was going to go into withdrawal. But you get used to it," Nat said. Part of the whole "embracing the great outdoors" thing and all.

"Maybe *you* can," Tori said. She sighed. "You're just more . . . *rustic* than I am, I guess."

Natalie bristled. She knew Tori didn't mean it as an insult, and she knew it was silly to compete. It was *especially* silly to compete over who was the bigger princess. But.

Silly or not, Natalie couldn't help feeling that her new friend, the one she had been so excited to induct into the cult of summer camp, was stealing her shtick.

Ridiculous.

"Maybe I just need a hottie trail guide," Tori went on. "You know, someone with great eyes. Like Simon."

"Huh?" Natalie said, feeling clumsy and inarticulate.

"Simon. I'm sure that getting lost in the woods with him helped you develop a new appreciation for nature, right?" Tori winked.

"Yeah, and, um, he's taken," Natalie said. "Sorry."

As soon as the words were out of her mouth, Natalie realized how much harsher they'd come out than she'd meant. What was wrong with her? So Tori was friends with a model; she was from L.A., Natalie could understand that—probably better than anyone. And Tori was getting along with Alyssa—that was a good thing. Camp was for chick-bonding; the more, the merrier, Nat and Alyssa always said. And so what if Tori thought Simon was cute? He was, that was for sure. She could hardly be blamed for noticing.

Tori chuckled lightly. "Of course he's taken, Nat. I was just kidding."

Natalie cleared her throat. "Right," she said quickly. "Me too."

But deep down, she wasn't so sure.

"You were born in San Francisco? I had no idea!"

"Yup, my parents were big-time hippies, back in their day." Simon smiled at Natalie, then shuddered. "It's very disturbing to think about my mom in a miniskirt with ironed hair."

"We can move on," Nat replied, laughing.

"Don't you think you've done enough probing for one afternoon?" Simon teased. "You've got my favorite color, my career goals, the name of my first pet—"

"Dearly departed Peanut—" Nat cut in, mocksomber.

"And now you know where I was born. You've got enough data for an *E! True Hollywood Story*."

"I just want to be thorough," Natalie replied. "I really want to run a piece in the Visiting Day newspaper issue, and this interview is like my audition. It has to be great."

"I just hope Jesse thinks I'm as fascinating a subject as you do," Simon joked.

"Who said I think you're fascinating?" Natalie quipped. *I mean, I do, but . . .*

"It's written all over your face, Goode," Simon said.

"It's nice that you're so confident," she said, trying to recover. She glanced at her watch. "Oh! Free choice is almost over. I want to go grab Alyssa before swim."

"Sure thing," Simon said easily. "Get ready for next week, when the tables are turned and you are subject to my inquisition." He put his index finger to his chin in a Thinker sort of pose. "I'm going to catch up with Ben and Gabe."

"Sounds fun!" Natalie chirped. It really did. Mainly because it was fun just being around Simon, no matter what they were doing.

She tucked her notebook and pen under one arm and wandered over to where Alyssa and Tori were sitting. It looked like Alyssa was interviewing Tori, even though Tori wasn't on the newspaper. It must have been just for fun.

But if it was just for fun, what was that slight echo of jealousy churning in Natalie's rib cage?

"Favorite flavor of jelly bean would have to be . . ." Tori drummed her fingers against the table and stared off at an imaginary point on the horizon. "Ooh—I love that buttered popcorn one. I mean, it really tastes like buttered popcorn!"

"Well, Alyssa won't go for that," Nat cut in, grinning. "She likes to keep her salty and sweet separate."

Alyssa raised an eyebrow at Natalie. "You don't

know *everything* about me, you know," she said somewhat pointedly.

Nat swallowed. Alyssa hadn't said anything rude or especially harsh, but, for some reason, a sudden chill had come over Nat. Of course she didn't know every last little thing about Alyssa. But they *were* best friends. That in itself meant that Nat knew a lot. More than a lot.

"Um, okay, then," Natalie said, making a huge effort to recover from the hiccup of weirdness. "So what's your favorite flavor, then?"

To Natalie's great relief, Alyssa broke into a smile. "Pink grapefruit. It's true. I'm a fan of the pure sugar rush."

Natalie giggled. "Simon likes that one, too."

Alyssa nodded slowly, collecting her own notebook and pencil. The cold freeze had come back over Nat. "Now, see, Simon you know everything about. *That*, I can believe."

This time there was no mistaking the edge in her voice. But Nat had no clue what to do about it. This was Alyssa, after all. They had never had a fight before. Ever.

"Um, what's that supposed to mean, Lyss?" Nat asked uncertainly. She looked from her old friend to her new friend. Tori, in turn, suddenly seemed extremely interested in her shoelaces. And uncharacteristically quiet.

Alyssa shrugged and ran her fingers through her inky, dyed-black hair. "Nothing. Never mind." She looked Natalie directly in the eye. "Let's go back to the bunk and get ready for free swim."

All at once, Nat was relieved Normal Alyssa—magazine-reading, horoscope-loving, free-swim-sitting-out Alyssa—was back. Nat was so grateful for this abrupt change of heart that she decided not to make a thing out of the random burst of crankiness.

Everyone's entitled to one, now and then, she thought to herself. *Right?*

▲ ▲ ▲

"Okay, so you have your pick," Natalie said. "Lucky us, I just got a brand-new shipment in from my mom yesterday." She fanned a handful of magazines out tantalizing them, like a card dealer at a casino. "We've got *People, In Touch, Us Weekly,* and—my personal favorite—*Star.*" She giggled gleefully. "Note that this may or may not be the very same photo of a certain blond pop princess on each cover."

"So, in effect, they're all really the same magazine," Alyssa noted drily.

"Well, sure, but that's that beauty of it. Multiple viewpoints!" Natalie exclaimed brightly. "I mean, you can't ask for more incisive coverage, right?"

Chelsea dropped her towels next to where the girls had set up camp. "Whatever," she muttered, managing to sound incredibly bored and totally irritated all at once. "It's so lame that you never bother to go in during free swim."

"Yup, we're lame," Alyssa said agreeably. She and Natalie couldn't have cared less what Chelsea thought of them. She smoothed a glob of sunscreen onto her pale shoulders and leaned back onto her elbows. "And we like it."

"Amen," Natalie said, popping a pair of over-sized sunglasses on her face. She poked Alyssa. "Warn me if I start to get that weird glasses tan, okay?"

"Definitely," Alyssa promised.

Chelsea glared at the girls and wandered down to the shoreline with Karen. The rest of the bunk was in the water, too—all except for Tori. She'd been joining them in their sunbathing more and more lately.

"Tori's taking forever to change, huh?" Natalie observed, flipped idly through a magazine.

"Yeah, I think she was helping Mia bring something to the kitchen. I don't know for sure."

"Speak of the devil," Nat said, looking up as a shadow fell across her torso. It was cast by Tori's tall, lanky body as she leaned over the girls.

"Here I am! The party can start!" she said playfully.

"We were just starting to worry," Alyssa said. "We wouldn't want you to miss a moment of celebrity gossip."

Natalie laughed. It was true, Tori knew a ton about Hollywood and could always be counted on to tell good stories. But . . .

Well, maybe she was being crazy—probably, she was being crazy—but there was a part of her that didn't want to share Alyssa with Tori. She felt like she hadn't had any one-on-one time with her BFF lately. And then there was that odd moment at the end of newspaper. . . . She and Alyssa really needed some quality time. But she couldn't just exclude Tori. Tori was her friend, after all. And, anyway, that would be just . . . rude.

"Goody!" Tori squealed, spreading out a huge, fluffy beach towel and stepping out of her flip-flops. She took off her shorts and T-shirt to reveal a very adorable ruffly tankini that did little to quash Natalie's mild waves of irrational jealousy. Tori was the picture of a cute California surfer girl. How . . . annoying. "Oh."

"What, 'oh'?" Natalie asked. "You've got your tabloids, you've got your sunscreen . . . where's the bad?"

Tori frowned. "It's just . . . I read those already. My mom sent them up to me a few days ago. They all contradict each other, anyway. Totally not reliable journalism." She turned to the girls thoughtfully. "I know it's everything we stand against, but it's kind of sweltering out here. Anyone want to go in the water?"

Natalie gasped dramatically and clutched at her chest. "Heavens, no! Do you have any idea what lake water does to my hair?"

Tori laughed obligingly, but Alyssa was busy shimmying out of her tank top. "Definitely," she said. "I am dying of heat." She looked over at Natalie. "You don't mind, right? I mean, more magazines for you."

Nat shook her head slowly, feeling a little bit horrified and sort of like she had stumbled into an alternate universe. Alyssa was spending free swim with someone other than her? Alyssa was spending free swim *in the water?*

It must be opposite day, she thought, the wheels in her mind clicking and whirring. *In the Bizzaro World.* "I don't mind at all," she said numbly, trying to muster up some semblance of a smile.

"Oh, good," Alyssa said. She quickly tied her hair up into a sloppy bun on top of her head. She gave Natalie a quick smile. "We'll be back."

She grabbed Tori's hand and the two scampered off, down to the waterfront, without another thought to sunning, magazines, or to Natalie.

▲ ▲ ▲

"Well, you look . . . thoughtful."

"Hmm?"

"That must be a *really* interesting magazine article," Mia said, smoothing out her towel and shaking her golden hair across her shoulders. "That's the third time I've tried to get your attention."

"What?" Natalie blushed. "Sorry, it's not, uh, personal. I'm just caught up in . . ." She trailed off, looking down at her open magazine. She hadn't been able to focus on a single word in the twenty minutes or so since Tori and Alyssa had gone off to be swim buddies. "I don't know," she confessed. "You caught me. I'm spacing."

"Looks like you've got something serious on your mind."

Nat regarded Mia. She liked her CIT a lot, but it wasn't the same as the relationship she'd had with her CIT last year, Marissa. She and Marissa had been bona fide friends, even with the difference in their ages. They still e-mailed each other, and Marissa could always be counted on for some great advice. Too bad she was in Big Sur with her family this summer. Natalie didn't know Mia that well, but Mia was definitely cool, and very outgoing, and in the week since they'd been at camp, she had always been there for the girls. Maybe it was worth a shot at opening up to her?

What the heck, Nat thought. It couldn't hurt, could it?

"You're gonna think this is silly," Nat said, hesitating slightly.

"Try me," Mia said encouragingly.

"It's just . . . I was really looking forward to coming back to camp this summer—and especially to see Alyssa, you know?"

"But?" Mia prompted.

"Things are a little weird," Natalie admitted. "Not exactly the way that they were last summer. I don't know why."

"Well, is there anything different about this summer?" Mia asked. "Anything specifically that you can think of?"

Nat nodded. "There's . . . well, there's Simon."

"Ah, the boyfriend," Mia said sagely. She shook her head. "So often the root of all girl issues. But you were with him last summer, no?"

"Not exactly. I mean, I was into him, but we weren't, like, boyfriend and girlfriend the way we are now."

"So, things have changed. They've changed for the better, in some ways, and really, we've all got to learn to go with the flow, but the truth is that these things happen. It's normal. Maybe Alyssa feels a little bit left out, now that you've got a 'thing' with a guy. Also normal. The trick is to make sure she understands that she's still your BFF. Even if you're splitting your free time between your girl friend and your boyfriend, you can still make sure they both know how important they are to you."

Natalie looked up at her CIT curiously. "You make it sound so simple. How do you make it sound so simple?"

Mia grinned. "I am wise beyond my years." She gave Natalie's ponytail a little tug. "Trust me, you guys have a true friendship. All you have to do is talk to her."

Listening to Mia, Natalie was inclined to believe her. She was older, so she had experience on her side. And she sounded so sure of herself, it was impossible not to get caught up in her enthusiasm and determination. She would talk to Alyssa. It was a good idea. Alyssa needed to know that she wasn't going to be replaced by Simon—or *any* boy—anytime soon.

Natalie glanced back down to the waterfront. Alyssa and Tori were barely within her view; they'd wandered off into the green water, which was the deepest end of the lake. A tiny prick of doubt pinched at Natalie's insides. She had been honest with Mia about Simon, but there was something she had left out of the equation. Because even if Natalie could be sure that Simon wouldn't interfere with her relationship with Alyssa . . . she wasn't so sure that Tori wouldn't, either.

There were no guarantees. At least, not until she talked to Alyssa. And put all of this ridiculousness out of her mind.

▲ ▲ ▲

Natalie didn't get a moment alone with Alyssa until much later that night. Tori had hung with them during siesta, giving out killer manicures and showering the girls in her newest batch of makeup samples that her mother had sent. Then Alex, Grace, Valerie, and Sarah had come by to play cards. And of course, dinner itself was way too loud and crowded for the sort of heart-to-heart Nat was planning. She finally cornered Alyssa on their way out of the mess hall, corralling her aside and letting the rest of the bunk speed up until they had some semblance of privacy.

"What's going on, Natalie?" Alyssa asked. "You're looking at me all . . . twitchy."

Natalie laughed. She *was* feeling twitchy, and it bode well that her friend could recognize that. Maybe this Talk wouldn't be too terribly painful after all. She looked at Alyssa shyly. "It's just that I feel like things are a little, um, off between us lately."

Alyssa's typically porcelain skin flamed crimson. "What do you mean?" she stammered.

Now it was Natalie's turn to falter. She had Alyssa's attention, all right—she just didn't know what to do with it. "I, uh, don't know how to describe it exactly, but it feels like it's a little, I guess . . . tense? Like there's something you're upset about that you're not sharing with me?" She took a deep breath. "I mean, if there is something, Lyss . . . you know you can tell me anything."

She paused, waiting for Alyssa to respond. For one excruciating beat, all Natalie could hear was the sound of both of their breathing and the scrape of their shoes along the dirt path. She thought she might crawl out of her skin if Alyssa didn't have a reaction, and soon. She tilted her head back toward her friend. "Please. Say. Something?" she begged.

Alyssa swallowed hard and took a deep breath through her nose. She looked for all the world as though she were gearing up to say something Important. *Thank goodness*, Natalie thought. *We so need to get to the bottom of this!*

"Here's the thing—" Alyssa began, her voice hushed and low.

"Natalie!"

Natalie looked up to see Simon sprinting toward her. Her heart leaped at the same time as it plummeted into her stomach. Was that even possible, biologically speaking?

"I've been looking all over for you!" he called, jogging over and breaking into stride with the girls. "You, like, just snuck out of dinner."

Perfect timing, Simon, Natalie thought. The last thing she wanted to do was to ask him—however politely—to go away. But, really, he couldn't have come by at a more inopportune moment. *You need to talk to Alyssa,* Natalie reminded herself firmly. *Don't let yourself be distracted by the cuteness of his . . . everything.* "Yeah, Alyssa and I were ducking out for some . . . QT," she managed tactfully. "Quality time. *Girl* time," she emphasized.

"Oh, hey, I get it," Simon said, so apologetic that Natalie felt instantly guilty. "No worries. I'll catch up with you at evening activity." He gestured to where two freckle-faced boys were hanging back, looking bored. "I think Ben and Gabe are ready to give up on me, anyway. They think I'm way too hooked on you." He blushed.

"I'm okay with that," Natalie said, thrilled beyond measure that he was being so easygoing about this.

"You know what?" Alyssa cut in.

Natalie's thrill began to shrink down from the size of a hot-air balloon to a teeny-tiny, shriveled raisin. "What?" she asked dully, having a pretty good idea of what.

"You guys talk. I don't mind. I'll go . . . find Tori, I guess," Alyssa said. "I promised I would do her left hand with 'passion pink' before evening activity, since she's a lefty."

"Are you sure?" Simon asked, looking very pleased with this turn of events. "I mean, who cares what Ben and Gabe think?"

"Right. I'm totally sure. It's not a big deal," she said. She looked at Natalie. "I promise." She turned and ran off without another look back.

Maybe it's not a big deal to Alyssa, Nat thought wildly. *Maybe.*

But she had a feeling that, at this point, she was fooling herself more than anything else.

chapter
EIGHT

Dear Hannah,

    Have I mentioned how much I love
Saturdays at camp? Sleeping in, brunch,
swim, and then we're free to do whatever
we want as a bunk until dinnertime. Bliss.
It's like the one time during the whole
week that no one's pressuring you to be a
big-time sports star or make lanyard key
chains or identify poison oak or whatever.
(Which, by the way, I am getting very good
at. The lanyard stitching, I mean. I'm a
little unclear as to what, exactly, a lanyard
is, or whose great idea it was to tie it in a

million different funky knots, but whatever.
You will be pleasantly surprised at the array
of lanyard-related gifts I have created for you
in my time in the arts and crafts shack.)

Meanwhile, you will also be glad to
hear that things are very good with Simon.
We've been taking the newspaper elective
together for free choice and we have been
interviewing each other as part of our first
assignment. So I have a great excuse for
being a nosy McNoserson and asking him all
sorts of personal questions. Good times. Don't
worry—I haven't gotten too inappropriate.
Yet.

My bunk is great. All the return
campers are finally getting used to being
split up, and I have to say, it's nice to branch
out and meet new people. Remember last
summer, when my mother told me she

wanted me to broaden my horizons? Who knew she'd turn out to be right? Crazy!

Well, our counselor, Andie, is very cool, though she's a huge jock, which is a tad annoying at times. I mean, her energy level is sort of scary. But I guess that's a good thing in a camp counselor. And Mia, our CIT, is great as long as you're not intimidated by the tall, thin, gorgeous type (which I am, but what can you do?).

I love the girls in my bunk—you already know all about the ones from last summer, and Lauren, Anna, and Perry are great. Anna is hysterically funny and scary-good at jacks, and Lauren can French-braid hair perfectly. I know, I know—you're impressed. And Tori—well, we have a lot in common. That's a good thing. I think.

Anyway, speaking of the girls, I think

they've got something planned for the afternoon, like a little party. Rumor has it that Jenna's dad sent up a crazy care package. The divorce thing may have been hard on Jenna emotionally, but seriously? She's making out like a bandit! You should see the stash of junk food she's got hidden under her bed. We're just lucky that she shares with her bunkmates so nicely... Probably one of the benefits of coming from a huge family.

I'm gonna run just in case I'm right about the whole party thing. Wouldn't want to be late! Hope you're having a fab summer. Don't miss me too much!

XOXO,
Nat

Natalie pushed aside the letter she had written to Hannah and sighed heavily. She knew she had managed to sound upbeat and cheerful in her note. Of course, she had left out the fact that she and Alyssa were in the middle of some awkward not-fight, and that Tori and Simon were somehow involved. She didn't want to say anything to Hannah just yet. Acknowledging the situation out loud would only make it more . . . real . . . and for the most part, Alyssa and Natalie were tiptoeing around each other, pretending everything was a-okay. Which it *so* wasn't. For her part, Nat was sort of miserable about the whole thing—but she had no idea what to do about it.

"Okay, so fifty-two percent of readers think that Tara Reid looked better in this dress, while forty-eight percent think that Paris Hilton rocked it harder. I'd say that's a really close call," Tori said, smiling and holding up a trashy magazine for reference. "Let's have a little 4A poll."

"Paris Hilton is gross," Chelsea said, barely looking up from the book she was reading on her bed.

"I agree," Karen said quietly. She did still have a habit of occasionally agreeing with Chelsea; old habits died hard, after all.

"I can't vote with the pictures so far away," Jessie complained, jumping off of her bed and scampering across the floor of the bunk to where Tori, Alyssa, and Jenna sat, Indian-style, on the floor. Jenna was munching away contentedly on cherry licorice twists.

"Paris Hilton *is* icky," Tori agreed. "I saw her at the Oscars last year and let's just say that she gets a *lot* of help in her paparazzi shots." She leaned in as if revealing a secret. "Airbrush," she stage-whispered.

Tori's been to the Oscars? Natalie thought. No way. No fair. She bit at a fingernail, gnawing furiously. Nat normally didn't think of herself as the jealous type, but for some reason, when it came to Tori, all bets were off.

"You were at the *Oscars?*" Perry shrieked, echoing Natalie's thoughts.

"Yeah, my dad takes me every year," Tori said. "Well, almost every year. He can usually get tickets from one client or another."

"So what?" Chelsea snapped. "I'm sure Princess Natalie has gone to the Oscars dozens of times."

"Oooh, have you, Nat?" Tori asked eagerly. "Don't you *love* all the fancy stuff they put in the bathroom? I get seriously overexcited about, you know, lip balm and stuff like that."

"I, ah, haven't ever been to the Oscars," Natalie had to admit reluctantly. Most frustrating, more frustrating even than the jealousy, was how genuine Tori sounded—she honestly wanted to chat about the thrill of attending the Oscars. Not rub it in Natalie's face or anything. Ugh. "Just the Golden Globes, once, when I was, like, five. I barely remember it. I'm not sure if they had any lip balm in the bathrooms. Those were my pre-balm days." She was trying to joke, but she didn't feel very joke-y on the inside.

"Oh, well . . ." Tori trailed off, obviously not

really sure what to say. Clearly she felt desperately sorry for non-Hollywood Natalie, whose movie-star father's connections were somewhat . . . limited. "Well, I mean, you're not missing anything. Just a lot of stars with double-sided tape on their boobs."

"Right," Natalie said. Stars with taped-up boobs sounded pretty fun, actually.

"Nat!" Tori called, startling her and pulling her out of her little internal pity party. "If you keep biting your nails you're going to wreck them."

"What? Oh," Nat replied, looking down at where she was indeed chewing furiously on the nail of her index finger. Gross. Natalie didn't bite her nails. What was going on?

How gracious of Tori to have my back, Natalie thought, a tad bitterly. She held out her hands, examined the damage, then silently turned back to her letter.

▲ ▲ ▲

Saturday didn't turn out the way Natalie had planned, at all. Simon had come by after the whole Oscar debacle, and he and Natalie hung out on the porch for a while. It was nice—Nat always loved to spend time with him—but she had really wanted to hang with Alyssa at least for a little bit, to try to get things back to normal between them. She thought maybe they could catch up during free swim, but Alyssa had gone swimming with Tori, which was happening more and more lately. "It's really hot out," she explained.

During dinner, Lauren cornered Natalie for

advice about a guy she was crushing on, and Nat could hardly turn her back on a friend in need. Evening activity was rained out. Indoor dodgeball. Highly conducive to a big-time heart-to-heart. Not.

Nat lay in her bed, tossing and turning, mentally running through the events of the day again and again. The flimsy mattress wasn't exactly the height of luxury, but tonight it was her thoughts keeping her awake more than any issue of comfort. Half the reason that she had come to camp was so that she could hang with Alyssa. She had to get things back on track between them. And Tori was . . . well, Tori was getting in the way.

Natalie felt horribly guilty to be as irked by Tori as she was. The girl was friendly, open, and outgoing, and other than her tiny faux pas on day one, when she'd ogled Simon, she certainly wasn't trying to offer Natalie any competition (and really, who could blame her for checking him out? He was way too cute!). But as similar as she and Tori were, it was kind of hard not to compare.

Natalie fumed silently, recalling how she had offered up her best YMs for lights-out, assuming that, as usual, her bunkmates would want to hear the trauma-rama column, and then their horoscopes. It was practically tradition, at this point—at least among the former 3C-ers! But just as everyone was settling in and warming to the evening ritual, Tori chimed in. "Wait," she said, perky as ever. "Why don't we do something different?" She pulled out a magazine of her own. "They've got numerology in here," she said.

"It's like astrology, but with numbers. Kind of cool, you know?"

And just like that, all of Natalie's bunkmates jumped on the numerology bandwagon, murmuring excitedly about how "awesome" it was to try something new. Like "new" was such a big deal. Whatever.

Mia and Andie had gone out after lights-out to a staff meeting at the rec hall. It was just down the path, halfway between the cluster of bunks and the mess hall. So it wasn't a big deal for them to leave the girls alone for an hour or so. "Just as long as you behave," Andie had warned as they headed off, the flimsy door banging shut behind them.

Natalie was contemplating taking out her flashlight and reading a little bit of the romance novel that Josie had sent. Would anyone notice? Chelsea might tell on her. Then again, with Chelsea, you never knew. She might be cool about it if it meant that she herself got away with staying up past lights-out. Natalie was weighing the pros and cons when suddenly—

"RAID!!!"

"WOO-HOO!"

"4C RULES!"

"You guys never saw it coming, did you?"

Stunned, Natalie sat up in bed so quickly that she banged her head against the top bunk. "What the—" she asked no one in particular. "Ow," she added as an afterthought.

In a flash, the lights were on and the campers of bunk 4C were weaving in and out of the bunk beds. They were cheering as quiet-loudly as they could and tossing toilet paper and confetti. They'd painted their faces in faux-camouflage, and the effect was startling. Alex and Brynn, in particular, looked very . . . intense.

"*What* are you guys doing here?" Natalie asked, finally wide awake and ripped from her stupor.

"We have to hand it to you, *Bloom*," Brynn said, shooting Jenna a knowing look. "That was pretty awesome, putting fake flies in our scrambled eggs." She made a face. "Gross, but awesome."

"We told you we'd get you back," Val put in.

"We figured we owed you one," Sarah chimed in.

"Yeah, we owed you one," Candace said. Candace had a habit of repeating what other people said.

"That's so stupid," Chelsea spat. "I mean, really. If you *owe* us one, why don't you *prank* us back? Not come by with"—she gestured toward the bags of what everyone knew were goodies in Sarah's and Tiernan's arms—"food and stuff. When someone pranks you, you don't throw them a party." She wrinkled her nose. Even with her nose wrinkled and nasty words coming out of her mouth, Chelsea was pretty. It really wasn't fair.

"That's exactly what I said," Gaby chimed in, looking sullen.

It was funny, Nat thought, to see the two camp bullies side by side. They were so similar and they didn't even realize it. But she couldn't dwell, she knew, when Jenna was reaching into her trunk and pulling out the mother lode of chocolate, chips, and pretzels.

"Listen, guys," Jenna protested, "I had nothing to do with that prank. But as long as you're here . . ." She rustled a package of potato chips noisily.

"Well, they surprised us, that's for sure," Natalie said, sliding out of her bed and making her way to the food without further delay. "And that's what counts. Let's eat!"

"Is there food for Alex?" Alyssa asked.

"Covered," Alex said, brandishing a small bag of what the girls knew was sugar-free gummy candy.

The two bunks settled into their impromptu party, laughing, talking, and teasing one another. Natalie was definitely impressed that her friends from 4C had managed to pull this off and keep it a total surprise until the last minute.

"Yeah, we had to wait, like, *forever* until Sophie went out. It's her night off, so even after Becky had gone to the staff meeting, she was hanging around and getting ready for some date or something," Grace said. She rolled her eyes.

"Oh, don't play it so cool, Gracie," Natalie said, laughing. "You know if you had a date with Devon, you might spend a few extra minutes gettin' pretty!"

Grace blushed to the tips of her earlobes, and the girls cackled. Devon had been Grace's partner in drama the summer before, and the two had totally crushed on each other. They weren't boyfriend and girlfriend the way that Nat and Simon were, but there was something there. Definitely.

"You should talk, Natalie," Grace said, smiling. "I hear you and Simon are in *looooove*." She made a kissy face and loud, smacking sounds.

"Come on—" Natalie said, starting to protest.

"—They completely are," Alyssa said, cutting in. "They're together 24/7."

The way she said it, it didn't sound like a harmless throwaway comment. Nat paused, wondering how to respond. Alyssa wasn't ever nasty, and certainly not on purpose. Maybe she was being too sensitive. Maybe.

But Nat just didn't think so.

"Girls! *What* is going on in here?"

The girls looked up in unison to find Mia and Andie bearing down at them. Their tone was stern and their arms were crossed over their chests, but their eyes were twinkling.

"Uh . . . it's a raid," Jenna offered. "And, for once, it's totally not my fault."

Everyone had to laugh at that, even the counselors.

"But I'm guessing that *is* your food," Andie said, pointing accusingly at the stash lying on the floor.

Jenna nodded. "Guilty as charged." She shook her head. "We had guests, I had to offer food. It's just good manners."

Andie gave an exasperated smile, but she looked amused. "Right, Bloom. Manners." She clapped her hands authoritatively. "You've got ten minutes to clean this up and return to your beds—that goes for the 4As and the 4Cs. I have a feeling Becky's on to you by now. If you can get this place back into the shape it was in before I left, and get out of here, we'll go easy on you."

Andie was being seriously cool. After all, they

could have gotten in a lot of trouble for being up after lights-out. The girls sprung into action, relieved to be escaping punishment. The stomachaches they would have in the morning would definitely be punishment enough.

It wasn't until later, just before she finally drifted off to sleep for real, that Natalie's mind wandered back to the comment Alyssa had made. Was she spending too much time with Simon? Was that what was bothering Alyssa? It seemed like Alyssa was spending just as much time with Tori as Nat was with Simon. Would they be able to get their friendship back on track before it was too late?

chapter
NINE

Like Saturday, Sunday at camp was a day of rest, where the schedule was relaxed and the girls could spend some time just chilling out, easing back into the week. Natalie had a feeling that the weekend vibe was as much for the counselors as it was for the campers, but she'd take it, no complaints! Any morning where she got to sleep late (if nine could really be considered late) was a fabulous, fun-filled morning for Natalie.

On Sundays, Dr. Steve skipped flag-raising and let the campers go straight to breakfast. It was his idea of "dispensing with the formalities," as though he never realized that nothing about camp was all that formal, anyway. No one minded taking a leisurely brunch, though. Of course, nothing that was served in the mess hall was exactly gourmet, but the cooks made an effort to do something special for Sunday breakfast: pancakes, French toast, and sometimes, when the campers were particularly lucky, something that didn't require any actual cooking at all (and therefore, couldn't be spoiled).

"Doughnuts! Awesome!" Jenna shrieked, seeing a buffet table set up along the far wall of the mess hall on this particular Sunday. "Out of the way, girls, I'm getting me a jelly!" She darted forward in a flash, her curly brown ponytail bobbing blurrily in her wake.

Everyone clamored to be first on line for the delicious—and thrillingly *non*-homemade—pastries. Suddenly a loud whistle pierced the air. It was Dr. Steve, standing on a chair at the head of the room, holding a clipboard and looking, for him, quite official.

"Yes, we're all very hungry and we all want to have a chance to get our first pick of doughnuts, but we're going to have to form a *single file line* at the buffet table." In response to the chorus of groans that rang out, he raised his voice. "I know, I know, it's a huge hassle," he teased. "But if you can't keep to the line, you will be pulled out of it, and you will have to wait until everyone else has gone."

Immediately, the campers fell into perfect formation.

"I thought that might be the encouragement you needed," Dr. Steve said knowingly. "Now. Announcements. First off, anyone who wants to e-mail his or her parents should talk to your counselor about setting up a time. I should warn you, it will mean giving up some of your siesta time, so please take that into consideration. Also, on Thursday night, we will be having our first division campout—so, fourth years, get set, because you're the lucky winners!"

Cheers erupted on par with those emitted for the doughnuts. This was great news—even for Natalie!

Whatever, she thought. *Last summer I learned to appreciate the value of a great campout.*

The value being, of course, time to hang with Simon.

This year, she'd actually know what she was doing. He'd be so impressed.

But—oh. This would be a great opportunity to take a step toward Alyssa, Natalie realized. They could tent together. She spotted Alyssa a few paces back in the doughnut line, so she sacrificed her own slightly cushier position for the sake of catching up with her friend.

"Hey, Lyss," she said, feeling suddenly more nervous than she would have expected, "maybe we can—"

"Natalie! We were just talking about the tent situation!" Tori said brightly. Somehow she already had what looked suspiciously like a glazed blueberry dough-nut tucked away on a small paper plate, despite being reasonably far from the buffet table. Nat's eyes almost bugged out of her head; blueberry doughnuts were her own favorite. They were also *very* hard to come by. "You *have* to be in our tent!" Tori continued.

"You—you want me in *your* tent?" Natalie asked in disbelief.

"Of course," Tori said. "You're, like, my soul sister here. I think you were meant to be my Girl Scout." She winked. "I hear you know nature inside and out."

Tori had misunderstood her shock, Nat real-ized. It wasn't that she couldn't believe that Tori would want to be in a tent with her.

Rather, it was that she couldn't fathom that she was being invited to join her BFF and another random girl—albeit a very nice girl with great fashion sense and a good sense of humor—as though she were some sort of hideous third wheel. She was mortified.

She looked quickly to Alyssa who, instead of rolling her eyes reassuringly or saying something normal, like, say, "Duh, of *course* you're going to be in our tent," just glanced downward. "Do you want to?" she offered halfheartedly, after an excruciating beat.

Did she want to? Natalie wondered. Not exactly. Not in this freaky, upside-down world where she and Alyssa were about as friendly as Superman and Lex Luthor. But she couldn't exactly say no. Saying no would be like throwing in the towel, quitting, giving up her friendship with Alyssa without even a fight. And Natalie for sure wasn't a quitter. Especially when her friends were involved.

"I'm in," she said, gritting her teeth determinedly. And marched off to find another blueberry doughnut.

Later that afternoon, the fourth division was involved in a heavy game of capture the flag. It was boys against girls, which was always good for drumming up people's competitive spirits. Jenna's twin brother, Adam, was guarding his team's flag very earnestly, making taunting faces at any of the girls who dared to get close.

Natalie hung to the back of the field, feeling

uninspired. She thought she might have used up her summer's allotment of athleticism the other day during kickball. So far this afternoon, Alyssa hadn't spoken much to her. Of course, a huge division-wide competition wasn't the best time to get all up close and personal, but then again, somehow that had never stopped them before.

Bored, Natalie let her gaze wander around the field. She saw Gaby and Chelsea huddled together, strategizing—though whether it was about the game or about how to terrorize their bunkmates, Nat couldn't be sure. She saw Sarah streaking across the green like her life depended on it. Another girl from her bunk—was it Abby?—was hot on Sarah's heels. Maybe they had a sort of bait-and-switch plan of action going on. She saw Priya guarding Jordan, as usual. *Just friends, huh?* she wondered. *Well, maybe.*

After all, right about now, they look a lot closer than Alyssa and I are.

All around her, Natalie's friends were Highly Involved in capture the flag. No one looked as quiet, moody, or—let's face it—as downright lonely as Natalie felt. Jenna and Jessie were screaming, tearing forward, and laughing hysterically. Valerie and Brynn were standing off to one corner, eyeing the boys' defense. In fact, the only other people on the field who looked as subdued as Natalie felt were . . .

Wait a minute.

The only other people on the field who looked as subdued, as intensely withdrawn as Natalie felt, were two people who, in Natalie's opinion, had no business shoving their heads quite so close together.

Tori and Simon.

What on earth could Simon and Tori be discussing so . . . *passionately?*

It's not enough that she steals my best friend? Natalie thought, fuming. *Now she has to go after my boyfriend, too? Nice.*

She was probably jumping to conclusions, she knew. In all likelihood, Tori was not after her man. So far, Tori had given her no reason not to be trusted.

No reason other than the fact that she has completely sucked up all of Alyssa's attention, Natalie mused, aware on some level that she sounded like a brat. She didn't care. She hadn't had a good heart-to-heart with Alyssa in days. That horrible, mean-spirited, spoiled-brat level was all she had right about now.

Natalie spent the rest of the game kicking idly at the grass and hoping no one noticed her complete and total lack of participation. Alyssa sure didn't, so that was one thing. When the game ended, Natalie glumly headed off back to the bunk by herself. She planned on taking a nap and doing a little well-earned wallowing all by her lonesome.

She didn't get far down the path, though, when she heard someone call her name. "Natalie!"

It was a boy someone, she realized. A Simon someone. She paused in her tracks. Did she really want to talk to Simon right now? She knew he liked her, but seeing him talk to Tori like they were BFF made her feel . . . well, it made her feel wretched, wrung out like an old dish towel.

You're being silly, she told herself. *You have to give him the benefit of the doubt. Get it together, Natalie.*

She swallowed hard and turned to face her boyfriend, pasting a bright smile on her face. She hoped it didn't look *too* artificial. "Hi!" she said.

"I didn't get to hang out with you during the game," Simon said.

I know, Natalie thought. *That's because you spent the whole time talking to Tori.* She managed to keep that feeling on the inside. But just barely. "Right," she said.

"It was a bummer," he said matter-of-factly. Just as easily, he reached down and took her hand. Suddenly they were walking and holding hands. All thoughts of Tori were summarily banished from Natalie's mind.

"Where are we going?" Natalie asked as Simon turned unexpectedly. Now they were headed for the lake, rather than the bunks. Did he think they were going swimming? That would be . . . strange.

"I just thought you might want to be alone for a little while," Simon said. "You know, just to chill." Was it Natalie's imagination, or did Simon's voice sound slightly shaky?

After a few more minutes of uncomfortable silence, Simon motioned toward a large, flat rock off to one side of the path. "Let's sit," he said.

"Okay," Natalie replied, still wondering why he was being so strange. They sat on the rock, which was cold. Simon continued to hold Natalie's hand, only now his hand was shaky the way his voice had been. And also, kind of sweaty. It was a little bit gross. But a little bit exciting. And also a little bit nerve-wracking.

Simon turned to look at her. He cleared his throat fairly ceremoniously. "Nat, I—" he started.

That's when it hit Natalie, all at once.

Simon wanted to *kiss* her!

There was no doubt in her mind that kissing was what this whole bizarre setup was all about. Why else would he have led her away from where the bunks were, when they were bound to get into trouble any minute now? And why else would he be nervous? Simon *never* got nervous; he was totally unflappable. That was one of the things Natalie adored about him. The shaky voice, the sweaty palms . . . oh yeah, it all added up to kissville.

Yikes.

Nat had never kissed a boy before, other than her father, or when Simon had kissed her on the cheek. For Pete's sake, she was only twelve—well, okay, almost thirteen, but still—this was uncharted territory for her. And she had no idea what to do. Did she *want* to kiss Simon? She wasn't sure. She wasn't even positive she would know what to . . . well, do, with her lips, that is, if she did want to kiss him. It was all very confusing and, unfortunately, happening in fast-forward.

Amid the swirl of emotions racing through her brain, there was only one thing that Natalie could be sure of: She needed time.

It was possible—not probable, but possible, nonetheless—that she was okay with the idea of kissing Simon. But that was just the very basic, bare-bones concept. If she was going to work her way up to actually *doing* it, well, she needed a second opinion.

A second opinion? Wait, no—this was bigger than that. There was only one other opinion that would do.

She needed Alyssa.

"I—uh, you know what?" Natalie asked, rising. "I forgot that . . . um, Andie asked me to be back at the bunk for something—"

"Oh," Simon said, looking crestfallen. "Are you sure?"

"Yeah, totally sure," Natalie babbled, backing away so awkwardly that she stumbled and nearly flipped over. "I'm, uh, going to get into trouble if I don't get back."

"Then you should go," Simon said, defeated.

"'Kay," Natalie said, breathing too quickly. "But I'll see you—"

"Later," Simon finished.

"Yeah," Natalie replied.

Then she was off.

"Please be there, please be there, please be there," Natalie chanted to herself as she raced back to the bunk. Her heart beat thunderously in her chest. Sure, things were tense with Alyssa, but that could be worked through. There were more important things at hand now.

Kissing things.

She threw open the door of the bunk dramatically, gasping to catch her breath.

"Slow down, speed racer," Chelsea said, barely

looking up from the letter she was writing. Natalie just ignored her. Quickly she glanced at Alyssa's bed: empty. Of course—Alyssa was sitting on Tori's bed. They were playing cards. Well.

All at once, Natalie felt shy about bursting in on their game, interrupting them. But Alyssa would get it, the direness of this scenario. Right?

Right?

Natalie quickly crossed the room to where they were playing, before she could lose her nerve. "Lyss," she began softly, "have you got a minute?"

Alyssa looked up at Natalie, puzzled. "But—I'm playing," she replied, gesturing rather pragmatically to her hand.

"Yeah, I know," Nat said apologetically. "But it's important. It's about Simon."

As soon as the words were out of her mouth, Natalie realized her mistake. Invoking Simon's name was definitely not the way to go. Alyssa immediately bristled, and though she recovered almost as instantaneously, her body went ever-so-slightly rigid. Just rigid enough for Natalie to notice the subtle shift in body language.

"Look," Alyssa said, "I get that Simon is important to you, but I don't think it's fair of you to spend all of your time with him and then expect me to drop everything when it's convenient for you." She didn't sound angry, just very reasonable and resigned. Almost alarmingly so. "Just the way I don't interrupt you when you're spending time with Simon, I don't think you should barge in when other people are in the middle of something." She waved her cards again.

Natalie's jaw dropped open. She wondered what the odds were that an earthquake would come and literally suck her down into the ground, just so she could escape the humiliation of this moment. Alyssa had seriously dressed her down. And the worst part was that she had practically no defense. There was nothing she could say. Her friend, always the practical one, was spot-on, as usual.

"I . . . I'm sorry," Natalie stammered. "I . . ." she trailed off. "Um, I guess you're right."

For a split second Alyssa looked almost sorry, and Nat wondered if they would actually talk things through. Then someone—probably Chelsea— snickered, and the moment was broken. Natalie felt tears prickle up in the corners of her eyes. Well, if there was one thing she would not do, it was break down in front of the whole bunk. She turned on her heel and raced out of the bunk. She didn't stop for anything.

Not even Alyssa dashing out of the bunk, calling after her, minutes too late.

chapter
TEN

The days building up to the campout were excruciating for Natalie. She had no idea what to say to Alyssa to make things better between them, so for the most part she just studiously avoided her ex-friend as best as she could without being too conspicuous about it. Though it was painful, it wasn't all that hard, she realized; she had come to adjust to the idea of spending her free choices, siestas, and basically the rest of her free time with Simon. When, exactly, had *that* happened? she wondered. No wonder Alyssa felt so rejected.

The worst time of day was free swim, when she and Alyssa usually went down to the waterfront to gossip and joke with each other. These days, Natalie and Lauren practiced their hairstyling skills on each other, which was fun, but totally not the same. Mia and Andie noticed that something was up, of course—they would have had to be blind not to notice—and they gently inquired, but Nat was noncommittal, not wanting to spill anything that might be construed as badmouthing Alyssa, and after a few attempts, the counselors mostly left her alone.

For his part, Simon barely seemed to notice that anything was up with Natalie. He was deliberately choosing to ignore the fact that she'd freaked out when he'd been about to kiss her, which was fine by Natalie until she sorted that all out in her head. But it was odd, she thought, that he was so oblivious to the Alyssa situation. And here she'd thought he understood her so well! But then again, maybe she was putting on a better show than she realized; she didn't want him to feel bad or involved or responsible for her state of mind.

Or maybe boys were just totally dense when it came to these kinds of things? Maybe he still had his mind on the whole kissville thing? Which, for the record, hadn't come up again. Nat couldn't decide whether or not that was a good thing.

The days dragged on slowly, mirroring Natalie's own less-than-perky pace, but somehow, before she even realized, it was Thursday morning. Very *early* Thursday morning. The girls of 4A—along with the rest of the fourth division—were loading their knapsacks onto the string of yellow school buses idling noisily at the front playing field, where they'd all been dropped off just—had it been?—just shy of two weeks ago.

"Everybody needs a buddy," Andie was saying a bit wearily. She was usually a ball of caffeine and fire first thing in the morning, but today she looked slightly ragged. Tiny corkscrews poked out of the constraints of her ponytail elastic. Nat had a feeling that being responsible for ten preteens overnight in the great outdoors could be a little nerve-wracking. She made a mental note to be especially nice to Andie for the duration of the trip.

"I'm going to get us a three-seater," Tori said, popping up like a sugar-rush victim. Unlike Andie, she was *incredibly* perky. Probably nervous, Natalie thought. She'd felt the same exact way this time last summer, when she'd had to go on a campout during the nature elective.

Natalie nodded numbly. She hadn't given any more thought than was absolutely necessary to the logistics of the trip; she, Alyssa, and Tori were still tenting together, as far as she knew. She and Alyssa were in a tragic state of forced, excessive politeness, which did not bode especially well for this trip. But who knew? Maybe they'd be forced to face off against the elements. Maybe they'd have to band together to combat rain, mosquitoes, and poison oak.

"Nat, I grabbed us a seat!"

Or maybe she'd spend the whole time with her boyfriend.

Alyssa looked off at an imaginary point in the distance. "I should . . . go help Mia with the sleeping bags." She wandered away, not meeting Natalie's gaze.

Now it was just Tori and Natalie. "You should . . . sit with him. If you want," Tori said quickly, shrugging. She looked guilty. But guilty for what? For crushing on Nat's guy? For stealing Nat's best friend? For being caught in the middle of not one but two triangles, even though she was, for all intents and purposes, a perfectly nice girl?

"Yeah," Natalie replied, feeling half relieved and half panicked. This solution caused almost as many problems as it resolved. But whatever. Her head hurt. She was taking the easy way out. She looked back up at the bus, where Simon was peeking out the window at her.

"Coming," she called, and jogged off to take her seat.

The good news about having a division-wide campout was that Natalie had all of her friends from last summer to keep her busy while things were so off with Alyssa. The two girls tried their best to be as normal as possible with everyone so that no one would feel uncomfortable, but it wasn't like old times or anything. The old 3C-ers were tactful enough to pretend not to notice. Or maybe they were just genuinely enjoying themselves, Nat thought.

They'd taken a hike, with Natalie and Simon acting as de facto tour guides, reprising their roles as survivalists from last year's campout. Only Chelsea bothered to point out that, in fact, last year, they'd actually gotten lost. "And we want everyone to see how much we've grown!" Natalie said brightly, ignoring Chelsea's sour expression. "I mean, I'm practically ready for Outward Bound now." The hike culminated in a visit to a breathtaking waterfall, where even Natalie conceded to strip down to her bathing suit and get wet. "This water is *freezing!*" Brynn cried—dramatically, of course—but it was the only complaint heard, and it was halfhearted, at that. Finally, the group made their way to a clearing in the woods that was to be their campsite. They pitched their tents, then headed a few paces southwind to picnic for lunch.

Everyone stuffed themselves on hot dogs or hamburgers, with Jenna and Valerie cracking jokes about the poor suckers stuck back at camp eating mess-hall food. "Yeah, suckers!" Candace echoed, enthusiastic as always.

After lunch, the counselors were going to put together a little demonstration on green living. Mostly it was a chance for the campers to digest and recharge, but there was a whole lesson to be learned about respect for nature. Natalie already had respect for nature—she'd learned it last summer, when she'd foolishly been separated from the group. She wanted a nice, long, respectful nap, but she had a feeling it wasn't gonna happen.

The afternoon sun beat down on her, and she decided it might be time for another dose of sunscreen. She wandered back to her, Tori, and Alyssa's tent. As she drew nearer, though, she heard voices.

Natalie didn't normally consider herself a snoop. But. As she edged up on the front flap of the tent, she heard Tori speaking in a semi-hushed tone. A semi-hushed, semi-*stressed* tone. Feeling slightly creepy but insanely curious, Nat leaned closer. Tori was speaking to Alyssa; Natalie recognized Lyss's voice. And she was talking about . . . well—with a start, Nat realized that there were only two words she could make out without question:

"Natalie."

And "Simon."

Shocked, Natalie coughed and stumbled forward involuntarily. Whoops. The outer frame of the tent wobbled.

Tentatively, Alyssa and Tori poked their heads out from underneath the nylon. One look at Natalie's crushed, confused expression and guilt erupted over both of their faces. Natalie had no idea what to say. Clearly they'd been talking about her. About her and her boyfriend. This was terrible. This was a hundred, thousand times worse than simply ignoring Alyssa, or even arguing with her. Knowing that her friend was talking about her with someone else—even without having any clue what they were saying—felt like a massive sucker punch to the gut.

Where was that earthquake when you needed it, anyway?

"Guys! Last one to the clearing is an endangered fossil fuel!" Andie called out, breaking the excruciating silence. Natalie coughed again, still saying nothing. And ran off to join the others.

ELEVEN

Evening activity was a bonfire. The counselors each took turns telling ghost stories, and then Evan, Simon's counselor, took out his guitar and led them all in some tried-and-true camp songs. Simon, Gabe, and Ben even did a boy-band-style dance routine that cracked everyone up. Natalie laughed despite herself, and threw her all into "Michael, Row Your Boat Ashore." *Anything* was better than acknowledging the hideous, crushing tension with Alyssa and Tori.

But she couldn't escape the two of them forever. They were, after all, sharing a tent. After teeth brushing and changing into their pajamas, the campers were all sent to their respective tents. The counselors would be keeping guard in shifts all night to make sure all the kids stayed in their tents.

Natalie had thought things couldn't get worse with Alyssa and Tori. But apparently they could. In fact, they could get much, much worse. Lying on her back in her sleeping bag, a thousand questions raced through Natalie's head. No one said a word.

Finally, she couldn't bear it. "Uh, Tori," she began uncertainly.

"Yeah?"

"Were you . . . when I came by the tent before, when I was looking for the sunscreen? Were you, um, *talking* about me, and Simon?" There. It was out. There was no taking it back now.

"Well, uh . . ." Tori hedged. "No?"

Natalie bristled. "Are you lying?" She couldn't believe it; she'd finally mustered up the courage to confront Tori, and the girl was going to outright deny it? Unbelievable.

"You know," Alyssa said, jumping in, "it's not a great idea to go accusing someone when you really don't know what's going on. And, I mean, why would you listen in on someone's private conversation, anyway?"

"I don't know, *Lyss*," Natalie snapped, dangerously close to tears yet again. She sat up. "I guess I'm just not used to us keeping secrets from each other." She couldn't help it—a choked sob escaped from her throat.

"Oh, hey—Nat—come on—" Alyssa began.

But Natalie was already gone—up, out, and tearing through the woods. She had no idea where she was going. Only that she needed to be as far away from Alyssa and Tori as possible.

"Nat! *Nat!*"

Natalie could hear Alyssa stomping through the

woods about as stealthily as an overweight elephant, calling for her in the loudest "whisper" Natalie had ever heard.

"Nat!" she repeated, more urgently this time. "You, of all people, should know better than to storm off into the woods by yourself!"

Natalie held her tongue, crouching behind a tree.

"And even if things are totally messed up between us," Alyssa called, "I have a feeling you wouldn't want me lost out here in the wilderness." She paused. "C'mon," she pleaded. "I know you wouldn't want that on your conscience."

Reluctantly, Natalie stepped out from behind her tree. "How do you know that?" she asked quietly.

"Because you're my best friend," Alyssa said.

Natalie sniffled. "It doesn't feel like that, these days," she said.

"I know," Alyssa agreed. She broke down. "Natalie, I miss you! Half the reason I even came back this summer was to see you!"

"Me too," Nat agreed. "I hate the way things have been. I hate this summer."

"You hated last summer at first, too," Alyssa pointed out in her own unique, matter-of-fact way. "You turned that around."

Natalie nodded. "Good point." It *was*.

"I think we just need to fix this ridiculousness between us. Then we can have an *amazing* summer."

"I agree," Natalie said. "I'm really sorry if you felt like I was blowing you off in order to spend time with Simon. I've never had, you know, a serious boyfriend before, so maybe I'm not so great at balancing my time. But you seemed, uh, perfectly content to be with Tori all the time. And so I got jealous." The words sounded ridiculous to Natalie even as they came out of her mouth. This was Alyssa, after all. Their friendship had always been solid. She should never have felt threatened by anyone else.

"Duh," Alyssa said, rolling her eyes. "But, I mean, what was I supposed to do? Sit around twiddling my thumbs? Tori's great—but she's not you. I had to do some adjusting this summer, myself."

"I get it," Natalie said. "And I'm sorry."

Alyssa smiled, looking incredibly relieved. "Me too," she said. The girls hugged. "That was horrible," Alyssa said, once the hug was over.

Natalie looked at her quizzically.

"Not the hug," she clarified. "Being in a fight with you. Or, a non-speak. Whatever the heck that was. Let's never do it again!"

"Hear, hear!" Nat said. "Let's get back to the tent before the counselors notice we're gone." She threw an arm over her best friend's shoulder, and off they went. Together.

🛖 🛖 🛖

Back in the tent, Tori was sitting up in her sleeping back, biting a fingernail pensively. "You're going to wreck your manicure," Natalie admonished, smiling, as she crawled back into her own sleeping bag. *Funny how a big, puffy blanket on the ground is more comfortable than a camp bunk bed*, she thought idly. Or maybe it was just that she was in the best mood she'd been in for days.

"You're back," Tori said, breaking into a grin. "All better?" she asked tentatively.

"All better," Natalie confirmed. "And, I apologize for being such a weirdo these past few days. It wasn't fair of me to be so jealous just because you and Alyssa were becoming friends."

"No, I get it," Tori said graciously. "I mean, you may not believe it, Nat, but I was *totally* jealous of you!"

"Me? Why?" Natalie asked, incredulous.

"Well, we're a *lot* alike, in case you haven't noticed."

"I had," Natalie admitted.

"Well, just think back to how you felt last summer, when you first got here," Tori prompted.

Nat reflected for a moment. "Shell-shocked."

"Exactly," Tori said. "I was so envious of how into camp you are. I mean, you never complain—not about the food, not about the showers, not about the—*ugh*—spiders on the toilet . . ."

Natalie paused for a moment. She almost couldn't believe it, but Tori was right. It was amazing, really, how far she'd come. "You're right!" she said. "Sorry I was such a doof. And for thinking that you were macking on Simon."

"Give me a *break*," Tori said, groaning. "I mean, he's really cute and all, but I would never crush on someone else's boyfriend. The minute you told me he was taken, I put it out of my mind."

"So, then, why were you and Alyssa talking about us?" Natalie asked shyly. She didn't want to dredge up more conflict, but as long as they were getting everything out in the open, she really needed to know.

Alyssa and Tori exchanged a glance. "I guess you have to tell her," Alyssa said, sounding *way* too serious.

"Oh, now you *definitely* have to tell me," Natalie said, eyes widening.

Tori sighed. "Okay," she said. "But just know that I really never wanted to ruin the surprise."

Natalie waved to her in a "get on with it" gesture.

"Simon came to me last week to talk," Tori said, sounding alarmingly serious. Natalie braced herself. "See . . . it's your anniversary, he told me. A year ago this weekend, you guys went on that nature campout."

It is our anniversary! Natalie realized. She couldn't believe it had gone unnoticed. The whole thing with Alyssa had really been keeping her preoccupied.

"So, he wanted to get you something, but he had no idea what you might like. And he knew that you and I had similar tastes. So he came to ask me what I would suggest."

Natalie's mouth dropped open.

"But . . . I don't know you *that* well, and I was deathly afraid of steering him in the wrong direction. So I decided to consult Alyssa, after swearing her to secrecy. We've been debating for a while now. We really wanted it to be a surprise, but unfortunately, as you're figuring out, it's kind of hard to keep a secret among good friends. Anyway, that's what you overheard before. Now that we know what he got you, we're *dying* for him to give it to you. You're going to love it."

"And I was so disappointed that you overheard us, after we went to all that trouble to keep it on the downlow," Alyssa cut in. "That's why I gave you such a hard time about listening in. I was a spaz. Do you forgive me?"

"Are you kidding?" Natalie exclaimed. She couldn't believe what amazing friends she had. Even when things were all screwy between them, they were helping her boyfriend out and making sure she had a special day. "You guys are, like, the best, *ever*. I won't even ask what you recommended to Simon."

"No way," Tori said. "There should be at least some element of the unexpected left. And you'd better act shocked when he gives you the gift, whatever it is!" She made a big, exaggerated motion of zipping her lips, locking them, and tossing away the key.

"Deal!" Natalie said. A thought crossed her mind. "Our anniversary! Maybe that's why he wants to, like, kiss me."

"*What?*" Tori and Alyssa shrieked in unison.

"This is what I was trying to tell you the other day when you were playing cards," Natalie said, giggling. "But you wouldn't be disturbed."

"Oh. My. God. You should have made us aware of the gravity of the situation," Alyssa chided her.

"Now. Spill."

"But, of course," Natalie said obligingly. There was nothing she'd rather do, after all, than have a nice, juicy, heart-to-heart with Alyssa and Tori.

Her *two* camp BFFs.

Second time's the charm, Natalie thought, warming to her story. *Totally.*

EPILOGUE

"How do you feel, Nat?"

"Does it itch?"

"Is your throat swelling?"

"Leave it to Princess Natalie to turn the camp-out into a high-drama scenario."

Natalie was propped up on no fewer than three fluffy pillows in the camp infirmary, soaking in the cool AC and the good vibes and well-wishes of her friends from 4A and 4C. Well, everyone except Chelsea, who could never resist a snarky comment.

Natalie had thought that the rest of the camp-out would be perfect, once she, Alyssa, and Tori had worked things out. Even Simon noticed the renewed spring in her step. But early on Saturday morning, Natalie's legs erupted in hives, and she broke out into a serious fever. It seemed that when she had run out of the tent and away from Alyssa, she had run headfirst into a raging patch of poison oak and was suffering a massive allergic reaction.

So much for my dreams of Outward Bound, Natalie

thought wryly. *I guess I still have a ways to go when it comes to becoming One with Nature.*

Susan, the head counselor of the fourth division, had whisked Natalie back to camp in her car, which was, not surprisingly, a much smoother ride than any yellow school bus, and Natalie had spent Saturday and Sunday in the infirmary with cold compresses pressed against her legs and hopped up on baby aspirin. Nurse Helen had even rolled an ancient black-and-white television set into Natalie's room.

All in all, it wasn't exactly the worst way to spend forty-eight hours. Ceaseless, merciless itching notwithstanding.

"You missed the *best* time, Natalie," Jenna said. "On Saturday night, someone snuck into the boys' tents and went through their backpacks. *And* they tossed their underwear into the lake. It *wasn't* me," she swore. She grinned devilishly. "But it was *awesome.*"

Natalie cracked up. "It sounds awesome," she agreed. "I'm sorry I missed it."

"We're sorry, too," Alyssa said. "I'd hug you, but . . ." She gestured at the compresses.

"Right, right, we need to contain the damages," Natalie said. "Wouldn't want to spread my cooties or anything."

Nurse Helen came into the room, waving a thermometer. "Natalie, this room's getting a little crowded, don't you think?" she asked, not unkindly.

Natalie grinned. "Yes, I'm stunningly popular. It's my cross to bear."

"We can take a hint," Grace said, pretending to

pout. She waved a finger. "But we *will* be back tomorrow," she said, making it sound like a threat.

The girls filed out, followed by Nurse Helen.

"Oh, Nurse Helen," Natalie called after her, not wanting to shout too loudly and irritate her throat. "What are the chances you'd bring me a cup of tea?"

"I'd say your chances are excellent. But, unfortunately, I'm not a qualified RN."

Natalie looked up to see Simon walking into the room bearing a steaming Styrofoam cup of what she knew was her favorite—peppermint tea. "Hey," she said, brightening at the sight of him. "I thought visiting hours were over for the day."

Simon winked. "Nurse Helen was willing to cut me a deal when I explained how our anniversary got busted up."

Natalie blushed. "I'm sorry I had to leave the campout early."

Simon glanced at the television set, and then back at Natalie. He raised an eyebrow. "No, you're not."

"Busted," Natalie said, smiling guiltily. "But I'm sorry I missed our anniversary." That much was definitely true.

"Well, I, um, got you something," Simon said, suddenly looking incredibly uncomfortable. It was adorable how nervous he was. Natalie had no problem whatsoever pretending that Alyssa and Tori had never given her a heads-up.

"A present?" she asked. "No way. That's too sweet."

He thrust a small, delicately wrapped box at

her awkwardly. "Tori helped me wrap it. And Alyssa picked it out. Well, she made the suggestion. And then my mom sent it up once I told her what to get."

"I can't believe you went to so much trouble," Natalie said in amazement. She fingered the box gingerly. "Can I open it?"

"You'd better," Simon quipped. "The suspense is killing me."

Natalie eagerly ripped into the gift wrap. "Ooooh," murmured, fishing out a dainty silver charm bracelet. "Wow."

"Do you like it?" Simon asked, sounding insecure.

"I *love* it," Natalie said. "Thank you so much." She held out her wrist. "Will you help me put it on?"

Simon leaned over and fastened the bracelet to her wrist. They both admired it for a moment, not saying anything. Then Simon broke the silence. "I'm really excited about our anniversary," he said.

"Me too," Natalie agreed. She couldn't help but notice that his face was very close to hers. Was this it—the big kiss moment? With Nurse Helen right in the other room? Was she ready?

Simon leaned in before she even had time to decide. Natalie squeezed her eyes shut, her stomach exploding like a packet of pop rocks. And then she felt it. Simon's lips touch down, ever so lightly.

On her forehead.

Natalie's eyes flew open. Her *forehead!* It was perfect! Simon wasn't ready for kissing yet, either. Natalie exhaled, only at that moment realizing that she'd been holding her breath in anticipation. She reached out and squeezed his hand, more sure than ever that he was, without a doubt, the sweetest, most perfect, most understanding boyfriend in the whole wide world. "Happy anniversary," she said, beaming.

"You too," Simon replied, looking quite pleased with himself. "Are you glad you came back this summer?"

"Are you kidding?" Natalie asked. "Second time's the charm."

Turn the page for a sneak preview of

camp
CONFIDENTIAL

Second
Summer

WISH YOU WEREN'T HERE

available now!

chapter
ONE

Hey, Diane!

I was so glad to get your letter
yesterday, you have no idea. And thanks
for sending the books—I've never read
The Phantom Tollbooth or Elsewhere, but
if they're as great as you say, I'm sure I'll
love them! I've finished up all the assigned
summer reading, too, so I've been looking for
a new book. I can't believe we're going to
be eighth-graders next year! That makes
us practically high schoolers! Can you believe
it?? I feel like we were just in Mrs.
Underhill's first-grade class, learning how to

sound out words and yelling at the boys for calling her Mrs. Underwear!

So how are things back home? Have you been hanging out with Taylor a lot? Are you and your family still going up to Lake Winnipesaukee this year? I never thought I'd say it, but I've been thinking about home a lot lately. It's not that I don't <u>love</u> being back at Camp Lakeview—I do. But so much has changed this year. Like I wrote you, they split up all the girls who were in my bunk last year, 3C. It's not so bad—we still all hang out together, and some of the new girls are pretty cool—but I still miss having everyone together.

And then, well—can you <u>believe</u> who showed up at camp this year? Maybe that's why I can't stop thinking about home—this year, "home" has come to camp. You'd think it would be nice having a girl from back home here at camp. We could tell stories about home, introduce each other to our new friends, and hang out. Instead it's just . . . I dunno . . . <u>awkward</u>. I try to be nice, but I really get the feeling she doesn't want to hang out with me, like I'm not popular enough or something. But this is <u>camp</u>, not school! ARRRGGH! It's so frustrating. Everyone thinks we should be best buddies because we're from the same town, but I think she'd rather eat bugs than be my friend. I don't know why. I've always thought she was sorta cool . . .

"Sarah?"

At the sound of her name, Sarah felt herself jump about three feet in the air. As soon as she looked down at the person calling her, she felt her face flush bright red. She knew there was no way that Abby could have known she was writing about her, but she still felt funny. She and Abby weren't friends, exactly, but they'd never out-and-out fought, either. Pasting a big smile on her face, Sarah shoved the unfinished letter into the envelope and stood up from the low tree branch she was sitting on.

"Yeah?"

Abby pulled her long brown hair out of its ponytail and piled it in a messy knot at the back of her neck. "Becky wants us all back inside the cabin," she explained, not quite looking Sarah in the eye. "She sent me out here to get you. They're telling us what free-choice activities we got this session."

Sarah felt her smile turn into a real one at that news, even though Abby turned around and started walking back to the cabin without even waiting for her to catch up. *Activities,* she thought. *Meaning hopefully, by this time tomorrow, Alex, Brynn, Valerie, and I will all be in sports together again. Awesome!*

Even though camp had only been in session for two weeks, Sarah felt like she might lose it completely if she didn't get to take part in some athletic activity very soon. Each session, every camper was assigned two elective activities, and Sarah *always* signed up for sports—along with Alex, Brynn, Valerie, and a bunch of their other friends from 3C. Last session, though, Sarah ended up getting photography and nature. And while she'd enjoyed them both, she felt like a piece of her body was missing. She *needed* to play sports. And this year—with Abby McDougal, Jock Extraordinaire from Sarah's very own middle school, not only at Camp Lakeview but in the same bunk as Sarah—she felt like she had a lot to prove.

Sarah ran to catch up with Abby, still wearing her big smile. Abby looked a little surprised, like she hadn't expected Sarah to smile at her. "So . . . " Abby said awkwardly, "what did *you* sign up for?"

"Sports," Sarah replied. "And something else. I don't remember. Sports is the most important."

"Really?" asked Abby. If she'd looked surprised before, now she looked shocked. "I didn't think you were that great an athlete. I thought you would have signed up for, I don't know—*newspaper* or something."

Sarah cringed. Abby said "newspaper" like it was the lamest thing imaginable. Abby was about the best female athlete at Winthrop Middle School, and since sports were really important in Winthrop, that made her one of the popular kids. Sarah didn't play sports at school, and was *not* one of the popular kids. She felt like Abby was trying to tell her she wasn't *cool* enough to play sports.

"*Actually,*" Sarah replied, "I really like playing sports at camp. Me, Alex, Brynn, and Valerie always sign up to play. We all try to be on the same team, and we have an awesome time together. Maybe we'll see you there."

Sarah ran ahead and opened the cabin door, letting it bang behind her. As she entered the cabin, she saw her bunkmates all collected in their bedroom, sitting in small groups on the bottom bunks. Abby followed close behind and went to sit with Gaby, and Alex, Brynn, Valerie, and Grace waved at Sarah and motioned for her to come sit down with them. Sarah shoved her letter into her cubby and scooted over to join her friends.

"Can you believe it's time to switch activities already?" Alex was saying. "I feel like camp just *started*. Pretty soon it'll be time for the social."

"Ugh, don't remind me," Sarah muttered. She loved almost everything about camp but, having zero interest in boys, couldn't care less about the social.

"Oh, come on," Brynn teased. "You don't know, Sarah. Maybe one of the guys out there has a *mad* crush on you. He'll watch you make the winning goal in sports and then run over and tell you how much he *luuuuuurves* you. . . . At the social, you guys can sit in the corner cuddling and talking about the Red Sox scores or whatever."

Everyone laughed, but Sarah felt her face start to burn. "Well, that's only if I *get* sports this session," she said, quickly changing the subject, "which I really hope I do. Plants are nice, but I can't deal with much more leaf rubbing and algae collecting."

Grace chuckled. "Come on, that was fun. Especially when you fell in the lake."

Sarah snorted, recalling the sample-collection-gone-awry. She'd come out covered in green goo and had to run back to their bunk to change while Grace tested their sample for pollution. "Yeah, fun for *you*."

At that moment, their counselor Becky walked into the room, holding a notebook and followed closely by their CIT, Sophie. "All right, guys!" Becky said with a smile. "Time flies when you're having fun, but here we are two weeks into camp, and it's time to switch activities. Everyone enjoy what you had last time?"

Most of the girls shouted "Yes!" or cheered, but Sarah was a little more subdued. "Sort of," she muttered.

Alex glanced over at her and winked. "We'll all have sports together this time," she whispered. "I can feel it."

Becky looked around at the girls and smiled right at Sarah. "Sarah, you're first up."

Sarah felt her heart start to pound as she got up and followed Becky into the small counselor's bedroom. It wasn't a *scared* excited she felt, it was a *good* excited. The last two weeks had been kind of weird, what with 3C getting split up, Sarah not getting into sports, and Abby, the biggest jock at Sarah's middle school, suddenly showing up in her bunk. Though she'd been glad to be back at Camp Lakeview, among her camp friends, Sarah had been feeling a little out of place—not the sports star she usually was at camp, not getting to hang with *all* of her friends, and not quite knowing how to approach Abby, who only knew her as quiet, bookish Sarah from back home.

But now, everything was about to shift into place. Sarah would be in sports again with all her buddies, and she'd surely impress the pants off Abby with her athletic skills, which would make Abby see how much they had in common and that they should be friends. Just like that, the summer would go from "okay" to "awesome." And Sarah could stop worrying about whether she fit in and just go with the flow, like last year.

"All right, Sarah," Becky said, sitting down and flipping open her notebook. "Good news for you, I think. I know you were bummed not to get sports last time, but just like I promised, I tried extra hard to fit you in this time. So you've got sports and arts and crafts, babe. You can thank me later—I accept cash, checks, and jelly beans." Becky looked up at Sarah and winked. "Just kidding about the cash and checks. But seriously—jelly beans are always welcome."

Sarah jumped up and whooped. "That's awesome, Becky! Thank you so much!" She threw her arms around her counselor in a quick hug. "I don't have any jelly beans, but if I come across any, they're yours. Thank you, thank you, thank you."

Becky squeezed Sarah and smiled. "No problem, Sarah. You were a great sport about it last session, no pun intended, and I really appreciate that. So have a great time, and send in Alex next."

"Sure." Sarah felt like she was walking on air back to the other room. It was amazing how fast things could start to look up! She walked back over to her friends and told Alex to head in to Becky.

"So what'd you get?" Alex demanded before leaving.

"Sports and arts and crafts," Sarah replied with a grin.

"All *right!*" Alex patted her on the back as Grace, Valerie, and Brynn all squealed their excitement.

"This session is going to be the *best,*" Valerie announced. "Just like old times!"

The four of them chatted about the year before

while Alex was gone, and when Alex emerged from the counselor's room and walked over, they pounced on her. "What'd you get, what'd you get?"

Alex shrugged sheepishly. "Nature and newspaper," she replied quietly. She didn't sound as disappointed as Sarah felt, but she didn't sound psyched, either. "Oh well. Looks like algae collection for me. Val, she's ready for you."

Valerie left, and Sarah scooted over to make room for Alex on the bunk. "That stinks, Al," she said softly. "Sports won't be half as much fun without you to compete against."

Alex grinned. "You mean *lose* against," she said. "But think of these two weeks as a practice time. You'll have two weeks to get up to speed, before we go head-to-head in the last session."

Sarah looked up and saw Val walking back from Becky's room. Her small smile gave away nothing.

"*So?*" Sarah asked when Val reached the bunk.

"Photography and nature," Val said with a shrug. "Oh well. I guess you'll have to kick butt for all of us, Sars. Grace, you're up next."

As Valerie sat back down and the discussion turned back to the social, Sarah tried to push back the rising panic in her chest. *Okay, so Alex didn't get sports. And neither did Valerie. But that doesn't mean it won't be fun! If all the other 3 C-ers were in sports with me—even Natalie and Jenna—it would still be fun. It'll still be fun, it'll still be fun, it'll still be fun . . .*

Grace came back then. "Nature and photography," she said with a sigh. "I don't know what's going on, guys. Why aren't any of us getting sports when it was our first choice?"

"It's weird," Alex agreed. "Poor Sars is going to have to play kickball or whatever with herself."

Grace rolled her eyes. "There *are* other campers besides us in 4C, Al."

"That's right," Candace piped up. "There're plenty of other campers. Like 4A and the whole third division, and the—"

"All *right*," Alex interrupted. "What I meant was, everyone that *matters* won't be in sports." She gave Sarah a quick wink to let her know she was kidding.

But Sarah felt herself growing quieter and quieter as the conversation went on. *It's true—nobody's in sports*, she thought when Brynn came back and excitedly announced that she'd gotten drama and ceramics. ("Sorry, Sarah," she'd said with a shrug.) *So I get to play sports, but I'll be all alone. Where's the fun in that?*

Gradually, all the other girls in bunk 4C went in to meet with Becky and came back out with either big smiles on their faces or the more surprised looks of not getting what they expected. For the most part, everyone seemed pretty happy—even Sarah's friends, though they hadn't gotten sports, seemed pretty eager to try out the activities they had. To Sarah's amazement, *none* of the other girls came back and announced they'd gotten sports. Between Gaby and Tiernan, Becky came back out to the girls' bunks and got everyone's attention. "I'm not done yet, but I heard some grumbling out here." Sarah and her friends exchanged guilty glances. "I know some of you are kind of surprised by not getting your first choice, sports." Sarah looked around the room. About half her bunkmates were nodding in agreement.

"I just wanted to explain that we had way too many girls sign up for sports this session, so we tried to move anyone who'd had it for the last two weeks into their second choice. Hopefully, next session, things will even out a little bit. So buck up, little campers." She grinned and returned to the other room.

"Well, that explains things," Alex said. "Sarah, you're the only one who didn't get sports last time. So you get it this time."

"I guess." Sarah shrugged. She didn't know how to say that she'd rather not have it at all than have sports without her friends.

As the last girl met with Becky, the rest of 4C started getting ready for dinner. Sarah ran into the bathroom, washed her hands, and splashed some water on her face. As much as she was trying to keep a positive attitude, Sarah couldn't help feeling like her great, everything-in-place summer had just been destroyed. *I'm going to be all alone in sports and arts and crafts. How could this get any worse?*

Sarah heard a whoop from the bunks and walked back out with Alex and Brynn. All of her bunkmates were standing in a group by the door, ready to go to dinner.

"So what'd you get, Abby?" Alex asked in a friendly way as they passed Abby and Gaby on their way out the door.

Abby turned to Alex with a big grin. "I'm so

psyched! I got nature and *sports!*"

Sarah felt her heart drop into her stomach. She'd been looking forward to being in sports . . . with her friends. Abby had been cold to her since camp started, and every time they spoke it just seemed to emphasize the fact that Sarah wasn't cool enough for Abby. Being in sports alone with her would ratchet the Awkward Meter up from 5 to about 5,000.

I don't believe it, but I think it just got worse.

chapter
TWO

"Okay," Alex was saying as bunk 4C strolled over to the mess hall, "so we won't have many activities together. But the good news is, this time every summer, the counselors start taking volunteers for the social committee!"

Sarah glanced at her friend and sighed. Alex had been coming to Camp Lakeview for years and years, and she always enjoyed sharing all the tips and secrets she'd gained as a Camp Lakeview veteran. Usually Sarah found that part of Alex's personality kind of funny. But in her current mood, it just annoyed her.

"*And?*" she asked. "And that's relevant to the whole activity thing *because . . .*"

Alex glanced back at her and pouted. "Well, if you'd let me *finish*, I'm definitely signing up for social committee because I want to help make sure this social is the best ever!" Her face brightened as she turned to Brynn and Valerie. "Not that it would be hard to beat last year. Remember that whole animal disaster?"

Sarah couldn't keep herself from smiling. The

year before, the campers had agreed upon a square-dance theme—and Jenna and Chelsea, in some fit of really awful judgment, had thought it would be a funny "prank" to bring real animals from the nature shack into the dance. At the time, it had been awful—the animals had panicked, the campers had freaked out, and mayhem ensued. Looking back on it, though, it seemed kind of funny.

"Anyway," Alex was saying, "*I'm* definitely signing up."

"Me too!" said Brynn quickly. "I think that's a great idea. And I have all kinds of experience with set decoration and lighting for the stage, so I bet I could really help out with those things."

"Me too!" squealed Valerie. "I mean, I just want to help plan the dance. Maybe make it a little more elegant than last year?"

Everyone chuckled. It would be hard to get less elegant than last year's disaster.

"I think that's a great idea," Grace agreed. "I'll sign up. Maybe Devon will want to go."

Sarah remained silent. She felt her friends all looking back at her, but she didn't say anything. The truth was, she'd rather poke herself in the eye with a sharp stick than spend all that time thinking about a stupid dance. She wanted to get to spend time with her bunkmates, but not *that* way. She'd go crazy listening to them go on and on about boys and who was cuter and who might ask who out . . .

"What do you think, Sars?" Alex asked hopefully. "All four of us on social committee? We'd plan a dance that would keep them talking for years!"

Without looking up from the ground, Sarah shook her head. "I don't think so."

"Why not?" asked Brynn. "I'm telling you, it's going to be *great* this year. And like I said, maybe there's a great sporty guy out there for you—"

"I said *no*, all right? I really don't care about the stupid social." Sarah's friends all stopped short in surprise. Sarah felt her eyes start to burn with tears. *I will not start to cry. I will not start to cry. I will not start to cry.* She'd spent the last two weeks feeling out of place, separated from her best friends, and freaked out that Abby had somehow brought all the stress of Winthrop Middle School to Camp Lakeview. Any day now, Abby might tell her bunkmates how *different* she acted back home—all quiet, a teacher's pet. Not at all jokey or competitive, like she was here. For the most part, Sarah was happy being sort of bookish at home—but camp was her chance to be anyone she wanted to be, away from the watchful eyes of her classmates. When she'd first tried sports, she'd been shocked to discover just how good an athlete she was. Even more surprising was how much fun she had doing it. *But now I'm stuck in sports alone with Abby,* she thought miserably. *I won't get to hang out with my best friends—they'll all be too busy planning the stupid social. Why did I have to be put in bunk 4C?*

She forced her way through her friends without looking any of them in the eye and plodded forward to the mess hall.

"Hey, Sarah! Sarah! Sarah!"

Sarah blinked and looked right toward the

sound of her name. Her friend Jenna, formerly of 3C and now of 4A, was standing on the mess-hall lawn surrounded by a few 4A-ers. She started waving crazily as soon as Sarah looked up, her messy brunette braid flailing as she moved her head to follow Sarah's approach.

"What did you get?" Jenna demanded before Sarah even got all the way up to her.

Sarah sighed. "Sports and arts and crafts."

Jenna's whole face lit up. "Awesome! I'm in sports, too. We're going to kick some boy butt!"

Standing close by, Natalie and Tori laughed. Sarah glanced over and saw that Alyssa and Chelsea were also there.

"I got arts and crafts," Alyssa added. "You and I will definitely have fun in that. I hear we're working with chalk pastels this session."

"Great," Sarah said sarcastically. "The only pastel I can pull off is if I draw a big mud puddle. That's what all of my drawings turn into eventually."

Alyssa laughed. "Oh, you just need a little technique," she said with a wink. "I'll help you out. And if I ever end up in sports again, heaven forbid, you can teach me how to land a slam dunk."

Sarah smiled. "Deal!"

Right then, Justin, one of the boys' counselors, opened the doors to the mess hall and all of the campers started stampeding in. Sarah drifted into the hall with the 4A girls, then split off and went to find the table for 4C. Sarah spotted Brynn and Valerie on the other side of the hall talking to a couple of boys, but Alex was sitting alone at their table, looking around anxiously. As Sarah approached, her face flooded with relief.

"Sars," she said as Sarah grabbed the chair next to her. "I didn't mean to make you mad with the social-committee stuff. And if you don't want to be on it, you *totally* don't have to. You know that, right?"

Sarah nodded and fiddled with her silverware. "I know."

Alex sighed. "I just . . . you seem upset."

Sarah sighed. She felt her insides turn to mush, the way they always did when she was upset and someone was this nice to her. She knew she'd been mean to snap at Alex. She didn't know how to explain that she was worried about drifting apart from her, Brynn, Val, and Grace, and all this other stuff. Alex seemed so confident all the time—Sarah couldn't imagine her understanding.

"Is it because you're in sports alone?" Alex asked suddenly, looking confused. "I mean Abby will be in there with you. She seems pretty cool."

Sarah sighed. *There's no way Abby and I will ever be friends, but Alex would never understand that.* "Yeah," she said finally, almost whispering. "I know it's lame. I was worried about being lonely, but yeah, Abby will be there, I guess. It turns out Jenna's in there, too."

Abby, Gaby, and the rest of 4C came over to the table and grabbed seats. Sarah watched them, not wanting to look at Alex and see if she understood. But she felt Alex reach over and pat her shoulder.

"You'll kick serious butt without us, Sars," Alex said confidently. "You always do."

Across the table, Gaby grabbed her silverware and looked across the room. "What's for dinner tonight?" she asked. "I'm starved."

"That's 'cause you barely ate anything at lunch," Alex pointed out.

Gaby shrugged, still craning her neck to see any sign of the CITs with their dinner. "Mac and cheese is bad for you. It's all carbs and fat."

"And *protein*," Abby interjected, unfolding her napkin. "And calcium? Honestly, Gaby, you're lucky you don't play sports. You'd run out of energy in about half a minute with the stuff you eat."

Gaby rolled her eyes. Sarah knew that if anyone else had made that comment, Gaby would have made some nasty retort. But since it was Abby, she'd let it slide.

"Whatever," Gaby muttered, smiling warily. "The point is, I'm hungry."

A few seconds later the CITs began serving the meal, and Sophie came over with a huge tray of meat loaf. "Gross," Gaby whispered as Sophie set it down in the middle of the table. "It looks . . . gray."

"Maybe it came from an old cow," Sarah quipped without thinking. Alex started laughing, and soon most of the table joined in. Even Gaby smiled ruefully as she took a piece of meat loaf and passed the tray around. The only person not laughing was the person who never laughed at Sarah's jokes . . . Abby. She just sat there, stone-faced. It was like Sarah's voice came out on some uncool frequency that Abby couldn't hear.

Nobody else noticed, though. Everyone assumed Sarah and Abby were old friends, since they both came from the same tiny town outside Boston. The truth, though, was that they ran in totally different crowds. Abby hung with the jocks, a bunch of popular girls and boys who sat together at a big lunch table and were all on the Winthrop Middle School sports teams. Sarah had only a few close friends, and they mostly kept to themselves. They were smart enough and well-liked enough by the teachers that some of the kids called them "nerds," but they got along with most everyone. They just weren't *popular*, like Abby and her friends. Sarah frowned as she watched everyone dig into their meat loaf. She loved coming to camp because she felt as if she could do anything here, and no one could tell her that she wasn't like that, that she was too nerdy, not popular enough, whatever. But she felt like Abby was always on the verge of telling her just that.

"Hey," Valerie was saying. "*You* got sports as an activity, right, Abby?"

Abby looked up. "Yeah," she replied. "I can't wait to get out there and play! Why?"

"Well, that means you and Sarah will be in sports together." Val nudged Sarah with her elbow, almost making her spill her bug juice. "See, Sars? You guys will have a *great* time together. Two amazing athletes from the same town! What are the chances?"

Sarah felt her face starting to burn. *She's going to*

tell everybody. Everyone will know I'm not really a jock. "Well, I'm not that great—"

But Abby was already speaking. "Yeah," she was saying. "Well, actually, I didn't even know Sars *played* sports."

Sarah winced. Sars was a nickname that no one ever called her outside camp. At school, she was just Sarah—Sarah Peyton, teacher's pet and all-around priss. Well, this was it. Sarah's cover was about to be blown. But she could out herself—she didn't have to wait for Abby to do it.

She put down her bug juice and looked Abby in the eye. "I don't, at home," she said simply.

Alex practically choked on her bug juice. "You *don't?*" she asked, slamming her cup down. "But you're *great,* Sarah! You're like the second-best athlete this camp has ever seen!"

Sarah raised an eyebrow. "*Second* best?"

Alex nodded, smiling. "After me, I mean. Well, maybe *third* best. Jenna's pretty good, too."

"You're *amazing,* is the point," Val chimed in. "You're such a great athlete! So why don't you play on any teams at home? It doesn't make sense."

"Yeah, it's weird," muttered Abby.

Sarah sighed and looked down at her plate. How could she explain it? The truth was, even she wasn't sure why she loved playing sports at camp yet never tried them at home. Was she afraid of losing?

"I guess . . . I'm just really busy at home," Sarah said. She glanced up just in time to see Abby roll her eyes, but she didn't think anyone else saw. "With schoolwork, I mean. And besides, camp is the perfect time to branch out, I think—to try something new." She caught Abby's eye. "With nobody judging you, you know?"

Abby looked away.

"But if you're good at sports, you're good at sports," Alex said, waving around a forkful of green beans. "Why not play on some teams? Don't you think it's a waste, Abby?"

Abby looked up at Alex. "I guess," she said, sounding skeptical, then glanced sideways at Sarah. "If she really *is* good. I've never seen her play."

"She's *amazing*," Grace said, shooting Sarah a big smile.

Abby took a sip of bug juice and shrugged, still unconvinced. "I guess we'll see tomorrow."

Sarah watched Abby as she lost interest in the conversation and went back to her meal. She kind of half-heard her friends turn the conversation, once again, to the social and what they wanted to do on the committee. Sarah guessed she must have looked normal on the outside, because nobody said anything to her, but inside, she was seething. *All right*, she thought. *It's okay that Abby doesn't want to be my friend, or that she thinks she's too cool for me, or whatever. But now she doesn't even believe I'm good at sports! She just doesn't think a "nerd" like me could be good at anything—besides taking tests!*

Sarah was finding it hard to concentrate on her meal. Abby's attitude was making her madder and madder. She poked at her meat loaf and shoved a few bites in her mouth before the CITs came around again to pick up the dinner plates. *I'll show her*, she thought, chewing fiercely. *I'll show her what a "nerd" can do. Tomorrow I'll blow Abby away at sports. If anyone can impress her, I can!*